THE GENIE FROM DOWN UNDER

Published in the UK by BBC Children's Books
a division of BBC Worldwide Ltd,
Woodlands, 80 Wood Lane, London W12 0TT

First published by Penguin Books Australia, 1996
Novelisation copyright © Amanda Midlam, 1996
Based on the scripts of the television series *The Genie from Down Under*
Copyright © Australian Children's Television Foundation, 1996
First published in the UK by BBC Children's Books, 1996

ISBN 0 563 40487 6

Typeset in 12.5/15pt Adobe Garamond
Printed and bound by Clays Ltd, St Ives plc
Cover printed by Clays Ltd, St Ives plc
Colour reproduction by Radstock Reproductions Ltd, Midsomer Norton
Colour printed by Lawrence Allen Ltd, Weston-super-Mare

THE GENIE FROM DOWN UNDER

Amanda Midlam

BBC CHILDREN'S BOOKS

Chapter One

Inside the opal, Bruce yawned and stretched. Beside him little Baz wriggled and fidgeted. They'd been stuck inside the opal for more than a hundred years. Baz was bored.

'Dad, can I go out and play?' he asked.

'No,' Bruce drawled in his Australian accent. 'Sorry, mate, but we're stuck here like dags on a sheep's bum.'

Bruce sat up straight. Something was happening. He could hear a strange rumbling outside.

'What's that, Dad?' asked Baz.

'Hush, Baz. I think I feel something,' his father replied.

Both waited expectantly. A white mist slowly filled the opal, and then they both knew for sure.

'Eureka!' Bruce cried, leaping to his feet. 'This is it!'

Baz stared at him in delight.

'I hope this time we get a good master,' he said.

The Honourable Penelope Townes let out a shriek. A strange mist arose from the opal she was holding. With another shrill cry she tossed the opal across the room. It flew straight through the open visor of an old suit of armour, and landed with a clunk inside the metal foot.

The attic of Townes Hall was a strange, dark place full of mysterious old objects. But an opal that emits vapours was just too spooky for words.

I must have imagined it, Penelope thought. She watched, frozen with fear, as vapours filled the suit of armour. A face-like shape began to appear mistily under the helmet.

Bruce's smiling face suddenly appeared.

'Yee haaagh!' he called. 'Anyone got a can opener?'

Baz burst out of the backflap of the suit of armour with a happy squeal.

'Dad, we're free!' he yelled exuberantly.

There must be some logical explanation for this, thought Penelope. Her body and her mouth were frozen in fear. She couldn't run, and she couldn't think of anything to say. But her mind was slowly working.

They must be paying guests, she thought. Townes Hall, her family home, had fallen on hard times, and her mother often took in paying guests to help pay the bills. But that didn't explain the mystery of the strange vapours.

Full of pent-up energy, little Baz rushed around the room like a whirling top. He saw a thirteen-year-old girl with long, brown hair, goggling eyes, and a wide open mouth. She was staring at him like a stunned mullet.

'Don't worry about us, mate,' Bruce explained. 'We've been stuck inside that opal for about a hundred and thirty years. We've gone a bit troppo.'

Penelope didn't understand a word. She heard the man say something about the smell of eucalyptus and wattle. A shudder ran through her.

They're Australians! That explained their uncouth manners, their stone-the-crows accents and the man's Akubra hat with its wide brim. But it didn't explain how they had suddenly appeared.

'Dad,' cried Baz, staring out of the window. 'I don't think we're in Australia.'

Bruce looked out of the window at the pretty English

countryside, looking so green in the bucketing rain, and his face fell.

'Where are we?' he asked Penelope.

'Aii eee!' she shrieked in fear.

'Aii eee? Where's that?'

Penelope backed towards the door.

'Where are you going?' Bruce asked. 'Don't be scared. We're just a couple of genies.'

Couple of loonies, Penelope thought as she continued to edge towards the door.

'You've rubbed the opal in your hand. Your every wish . . .' began Baz, making big, bold hand gestures.

This was too much for Penelope. With a scream she rushed out through the door and slammed it behind her. Baz was extremely disappointed. He was a junior genie, just learning to use his magic. He would have liked to practise on Penelope.

'Don't worry, son,' Bruce reassured him. 'The way you said it was just perfect.'

'Maybe my hand actions were too much,' Baz mumbled.

Bruce and Baz slid their heads effortlessly through the closed door. Penelope, trying to convince herself that she was dreaming, watched in horror.

'What my son was trying to say . . .' Bruce said cheerfully.

Penelope blinked at him in terror. Then she screamed and ran off down the corridor, yelling for her mother. Bruce looked at Baz sadly. 'I don't think it was the hand actions.'

Downstairs, Penelope's mother, Lady Diana Townes, heard the screams and rushed upstairs, followed closely by Mossop, the housekeeper.

'Darling, what is it?' cried Diana.

Penelope gulped for air and tried to explain that two Australians were in the attic. 'Their heads came through the door,' she squealed.

Mossop bravely took off one shoe to use as a weapon, and crept towards the attic door.

'I can't see any Australians,' she called a moment later.

Penelope peeked around the door. Sure enough, the Australians were gone.

'I think you'd better have a lie down before the wedding. You're a bit over-excited,' Mossop said, leading Penelope away.

Diana sighed deeply. It was her wedding day. She was going to marry Lord Akryngton-Smythe, whom everyone called Bubbles. There were flowers to be arranged, and guests were due to arrive, but more than anything she longed for a moment to herself. Quietly she went to her bedroom.

Bruce and Baz appeared invisibly beside her and Bruce gazed at Diana's beautiful but sad face.

'She's nice,' Baz said approvingly, in a voice that Diana couldn't hear. He didn't remember his own mother, and his face was wistful as he looked at Diana.

'Yeah,' Bruce muttered. He was also impressed with Diana. Not only was she beautiful but she seemed so much nicer than her screaming daughter. 'Wouldn't it be great if she was our master?'

Then Diana left the bedroom, so Bruce and Baz materialised fully. They stood looking out the window.

'Brrr. I'm cold, Dad. Where are we?'

'I think we're in Pommyland. But don't worry, we'll soon be on our way home,' Bruce said confidently.

Penelope lay in bed thinking, and listening to the rain drumming down outside. Her mother was about to marry Bubbles, who was stinking rich. Once Penelope had a rich stepfather, shabby Townes Hall would be restored to its former glory. And she, Penelope, would have everything she wanted. As she idly toyed with the opal pendant she thought of all the things she'd like to have.

'Ah, there you are,' said Baz in a friendly voice. 'Here she is, Dad!'

Penelope watched as Bruce materialised in front of her eyes. There was no denying that something strange was going on. She peered at Bruce and Baz cautiously. She had no idea who or what they were, but she knew one thing for sure. She was English and therefore she was superior.

'Who are you? And what do you want?' she demanded.

'My name's Bruce. I'm a genie and this is my son,' Bruce explained. 'His name is Barry but I call him Baz.'

Baz had never seen a television set or modern toys before. His eyes lit up. Happily he started playing with Penelope's things. He had no idea where he was, but it was better than being trapped in a boring opal.

Bruce looked at Penelope. She looked back at him steadily with a haughty look on her face.

'You're the master. Your every wish is our command,' he told her casually. 'You've got one complete day of unlimited wishing. Then you have to send us back to Australia and set us free. It's pretty straightforward. Any questions?'

He hoped she wouldn't have any. Over thousands of years, Bruce had become bored explaining genie rules to new masters. But Penelope had a whole bunch of questions.

'Why an opal?' she asked. 'Genies are supposed to be in lamps, aren't they?'

'The Grand Magician was a bit cheesed off with me,' Bruce explained. 'So he sent me and the boy into the middle of that opal, in the middle of a mine, in the middle of a desert, in the middle of that great south land, Australia. He thought we'd never get out.'

'So what are you doing in Wiltshire?' Penelope asked. Her crisp English accent was in broad contrast to Bruce's flat tones.

'A Pommy bloke called Claude Townes found us,' Bruce said.

'I'll have you know that *Sir* Claude Townes was my great-great-great-grandfather,' Penelope said snobbishly.

'He was always a bit of a pinhead,' said Bruce cheerfully.

'You're very disrespectful,' Penelope retorted. It was time to put Bruce in his place. 'Anyway, I don't believe that you are a genie.'

'Fair enough. No skin off my nose.' Bruce looked like he couldn't care less. 'Just say, "I wish you were back in Australia right now," and we'll be off like a bucket of prawns in the sun. We'll never bother you again.'

Penelope considered it. If that's what it would take to get

rid of these rude Australians, maybe she'd do it. Just then there was a knock at her bedroom door.

'Penelope?' Bubbles called from the corridor.

'Just say it, mate, and we'll be gone,' Bruce urged.

Penelope looked at him suspiciously. Why was he in such a hurry?

'Hang around,' she said bossily.

Both Bruce and Baz looked disappointed. 'Is that a wish?' Bruce asked.

'Yes,' replied Penelope. Bruce swatted the air, as if he was swatting a fly, and suddenly he and Baz were hanging upside-down from the ceiling.

'What are you doing up there?' Penelope asked, her mouth hanging open.

'Hanging around,' Baz explained.

'That was your wish,' Bruce added.

'Penelope. Are you all right?' Bubbles called. He sounded concerned. Penelope stared at Bruce and Baz.

'Get down from there,' she hissed at them. 'I wish you'd just disappear.'

Bruce swatted the air and the genies vanished.

'If you want me to go away, I understand,' Bubbles called. 'But I was rather hoping we could have a chat.'

Penelope went to the door and opened it for him.

'I wasn't talking to you,' she explained. Bubbles looked round the room in confusion. He couldn't see anyone in the room apart from Penelope.

'Is this the bloke your Mum's marrying?' asked the invisible Bruce. He couldn't believe that Diana would marry such a complete and utter prat.

'Will you be quiet!' Penelope said determinedly. Bubbles looked at her strangely, assuming she was talking to him.

'I'm sorry,' Penelope muttered. 'I'm not talking to you.'

Bubbles smiled weakly at her. He had no children of his own and assumed that all teenagers were strange. He was here on a mission. In his bumbling way, he tried to reassure Penelope that he'd be a good stepfather.

'You probably think I'm an old fuddy-duddy,' he said. 'But really I can be quite hip. A cool dude.'

Bubbles was a total rambling idiot, but Penelope smiled.

'Bubbles, I'm thrilled you and Mummy are getting married,' Penelope assured him. 'I think you'll be a smashing daddy.'

Bubbles was very relieved. 'Thank you, Penelope. That's what I wanted to hear. I've been so worried, so uptight.'

'If I was you I'd be worried too,' Bruce muttered.

'Will you keep quiet!' hissed Penelope.

'It's okay, I understand,' Bubbles told her. 'I know you're not talking to me.'

He had no idea who she was talking to, but that didn't bother him. As long as Penelope was happy to have him as her stepfather, that was all that mattered. Happily he shook her hand and left the room.

'Your mum's marrying *him*?' Bruce asked in disbelief.

'That's right,' Penelope informed him. 'They're in love.'

'I reckon he's a few sheep short in the top paddock,' said Baz.

Penelope suspected this meant that Bubbles was lacking in brain cells. This was true, but it was beside the point. He would make a wonderful, and very wealthy, stepfather.

Penelope pondered the major changes in her life as she dressed up for the wedding and did her hair. It looked like she was gaining a rich stepfather *and* two genies to boss around, all in one day. That is, if they really were genies. The best thing to do, she decided, was to test them. Thoughtfully she rubbed the opal and Bruce and Baz appeared before her.

'I'm not saying that I believe you're genies,' she told them. 'But if you are, would you be able to grant a wish? If I wished for a beautiful day for Mummy's wedding, would you be able to do it?'

'Yeah,' Bruce said flatly. Her snobbish manner irritated him and his face betrayed his feelings, but she was his master. 'We should be able to rustle up a few rays for you.'

'Well then,' Penelope said grandly. 'I wish it was a beautiful day.'

Bruce and Baz both swatted. The rain stopped suddenly and dazzling sunshine flooded the garden. Penelope, looking through the window, was impressed, but she refused to admit it.

'That should make my mother happy,' she said.

'She'll never be happy if she has to marry that Booby bloke,' Baz told her solemnly.

'His name is Bubbles,' Penelope said airily. 'He happens to be one of the richest men in England. And Mummy is going to be very, very happy. So there.'

'She's only doing it for you,' Bruce said gruffly.

Penelope was scornful. 'Don't be ridiculous. She's in love.'

Bruce decided to give it to her straight. 'If you could be

a fly on the wall right now, you'd realise just how unhappy your mother really is.'

'Is that so?' Penelope retorted. 'Well, I wish I *was* a fly on the wall right now, just so I could prove you wrong.'

Bruce smiled mischievously. As he began to swat the air, Penelope realised that she'd made a wish she didn't really want. But it was too late.

'You tricked me,' Penelope buzzed, her voice coming out in a tiny shriek. She, Bruce and Baz had been transformed into three flies on a wall in the library, where Diana was conferring with Mossop about the catering arrangements.

'He loves curry,' said Mossop. But Diana's thoughts were off on another track.

'I don't love him, Mossie,' she said quietly. 'I don't think I can go through with it.'

Penelope, staring down at her mother from a dizzying height, was astounded. Her mother's real feelings were a complete and unpleasant surprise to her.

'But . . .' Penelope started to squeak.

Mossop spotted the flies on the wall. She rolled up a newspaper to use as a weapon as she continued the conversation.

'Your Ladyship, I don't see that you have any choice. It's too late. The guests are already on their way. You have to marry Lord Akryngton-Smythe. For the sake of Townes Hall. For Penelope . . .'

'I didn't know,' Penelope squeaked. She felt like crying.

Mossop suddenly swatted at the flies. Penelope, Bruce and Baz realised they'd better get out of there before they were squashed.

Back in her room, Penelope couldn't bear the way Bruce and Baz looked at her. They obviously felt sorry for her and she hated them seeing her distress.

'Please,' she said. 'I think I want to be alone.'

Bruce nodded at Baz and they disappeared. Penelope, chastened by her new understanding of the situation, thought for a minute then quietly climbed the stairs to the attic. There she found two books she remembered seeing in her great-great-great-grandfather's trunk. One was his diary, and the other was a book about genies.

In the Townes Hall chapel the wedding guests were wilting. The weather had suddenly become unseasonably warm, and only Bruce and Baz felt comfortable in the heat. Guests fidgeted restlessly as the organist played the same music over again. It was fashionable for the bride to be late, but that wasn't the reason the wedding was delayed. Penelope, the maid of honour, was missing.

Diana poked her head inside the chapel and saw Bubbles pointing at his watch and signalling to her. Diana sighed. She had no idea where Penelope was. They had waited as long as they could. Sombrely she nodded to Bubbles, who nodded to the minister, who signalled the organist, who started playing 'Here Comes the Bride'.

Diana came down the aisle with Mossop as a last-minute replacement for Penelope. Bruce's heart went out to Diana, and her eyes met his briefly as she passed his pew. Halfway through the ceremony, Penelope quietly appeared at the door of the chapel.

'If any man can show just cause why they may not lawfully be joined together . . .' she heard the minister say, ' . . . let him speak now or else hereafter forever hold his peace.'

'I object!' said Penelope loudly and clearly. The wedding guests gasped and Diana, Bubbles and Mossop looked shocked. Only Bruce and Baz looked pleased. There was total consternation as the wedding service ground to a halt.

'I've never been so humiliated in my life,' Diana fumed as she strode across the green lawn leading from the chapel to the front door of Townes Hall. Penelope trailed along beside her, wondering how to explain.

'I beg your pardon,' Diana said as she bumped into Bruce, who appeared from behind a large stone column.

'No worries,' replied Bruce, smiling at her.

Diana gazed at him steadily. His blue eyes and friendly face were appealing but she had no idea who he was.

'Aren't you going to introduce us, Pen?' Bruce asked.

Diana turned to Penelope in surprise. 'You know this gentleman?'

Penelope frowned. She didn't want to introduce them, but she had no choice.

'He's Australian. His name is Bruce. And this is his son Barry.'

'Just call me Baz,' the little boy smiled. His father grinned even more broadly at Diana.

'Are you in charge of the marquee, Bruce?' Diana asked with quiet dignity. 'Take it down please. We won't be needing it.'

Diana led Penelope away for a private conversation and Penelope's heart sank. She was sure her mother was going to blast her. But Diana gazed around at the sunshine and gave her a rueful smile.

'It's turned out to be a nice day after all. Thank you, darling. Somehow you did the wrong thing at the right time. The question now is – how on earth are we going to keep Townes Hall?'

Penelope had ideas about that. 'Don't worry, Mummy,' she said happily. 'Something will turn up.'

A little later on, Penelope walked jubilantly into the stables. In her hands she carried the genie book and Sir Claude Townes's diary.

'I'm proud of you, mate,' Bruce told her, genuinely happy to see that at heart she was a good person. Penelope smiled at him.

'Thank you,' she replied. 'It wasn't a hard decision. After all, we don't need Bubbles' money any more – not when I've got you.'

Baz was playing with Penelope's horse Jumpy. He looked up at Bruce questioningly. Bruce looked at the books Penelope was carrying and grimaced.

'I don't have you for just one day,' Penelope informed him knowingly. 'I can have you for as long as I like. And I don't ever have to set you free if I don't feel like it.'

'It looks like she's on to us, Dad,' Baz mumbled.

'You can't even hold the opal,' Penelope said. To demonstrate her knowledge of genies she dropped the opal into Bruce's hand, and it slipped straight through his palm.

'Fair enough, Pen,' Bruce said in his easygoing way. Then he added casually, 'Have you ever wanted to go to Australia?'

Penelope cut him short.

'I have no intention of going to Australia,' she said scornfully, then added with a shudder, 'I wouldn't be seen dead down there. The very idea of it makes me sick.'

Bruce and Baz looked very glum at the thought of never seeing their homeland again. But Penelope didn't care. She was excited about her own plans.

'I want to make some wishes now,' she said imperiously. 'First of all I want to be rich. I want to be a woman of property.'

'How much would you like to be worth?' Bruce asked. Penelope was aware that his clear blue eyes seemed to be appraising her.

'I won't be greedy,' she replied haughtily. 'Twenty million pounds will do.'

Bruce smiled at her, a long, lazy, drawn-out smile. Then he swatted.

This is going to be great, thought Penelope. She closed her eyes and hugged herself in excitement at the thought of the wish coming true.

Chapter Two

Penelope opened her eyes and hugged herself with horror. Her beloved green English countryside had vanished. In its place was a wide brown featureless land stretching to the horizon.

Penelope shivered despite the relentless heat of the bright sun in the cloudless sky. Beside her, her mother and Mossop were jumping with excitement.

'Here are the deeds to the property!' Diana almost sang, she was so happy.

'Property. What property?' Penelope asked, stunned.

'Townes Downs. The property you've just inherited Down Under,' said Mossop.

'Down under what?' Penelope asked, hoping there was some mistake.

'Here in Australia, silly,' Mossop replied cheerfully.

'Five hundred square miles!' Diana sighed happily. 'Isn't it exciting!'

'How much is it worth?' Penelope asked faintly. She suspected she already knew the answer.

'Twenty million pounds,' Mossop told her joyfully.

In dismay Penelope turned around and saw the homestead. It was a dilapidated ramshackle building of peeling paint and termite-riddled timber. Bruce and Baz lounged on the verandah, happy to be home. Cheerfully they waved to her.

Penelope smiled slowly. She had the opal. She could make another wish. Quickly she marched up to Bruce.

'I've got the opal,' she said in a steely voice. 'I'm the

master and I'm going to wish us all back to civilisation right now.'

'Calm down, mate. You're in Australia,' Bruce drawled languidly.

'I am calm,' Penelope shrieked.

Diana came running.

'Is something wrong, darling?' she asked.

'Yes, there is,' Penelope replied as she struggled to maintain her cool. 'I want to go home to England right now. Don't you?'

'Actually, no. I quite like it here,' Diana commented. Penelope was aghast but Bruce and Baz just smiled.

'All right,' Penelope told the genies crossly as she surveyed the litter and junk scattered in her new bedroom. 'We shan't be going back to England just yet. But I've still got the opal and I'm the master. Now I wish you to clear out this room.'

'I can do that,' Baz said helpfully and swatted the air.

All the junk, plus Penelope, flew through the air and landed in a rubbish heap outside. Penelope pulled off a lampshade that had landed on her head, then picked herself up and dusted herself off. Bruce and Baz watched her through the window, laughing.

Penelope stormed back inside.

'I've had just about enough of you,' she yelled. 'I'm the master. In fact, you said you were my slaves.'

Bruce remained unperturbed and Penelope glared at him.

'I think it's time you started behaving like a slave,'

Penelope said in fury, unaware that her mother and Mossop had entered the room. 'I think it's time you showed some respect for your master.'

Diana gasped in shock. She herself had been raised to remain polite at all times, and she'd tried to bring Penelope up with the same good manners. Penelope realised her mother and Mossop had heard every word. She tried to explain.

'Mummy, you don't understand. He's not really human . . .'

Diana looked more shocked than ever and Mossop quickly chided Penelope.

'Just because he's Australian, it doesn't mean he's not human.'

'Penelope, I'm shocked,' Diana said disapprovingly. 'How can you justify such rude behaviour?'

'Don't worry about it, mate,' Bruce said with a grin. He pretended to notice her opal. 'Hey, is that a black opal?'

Diana reached out to touch the opal hanging on a chain around Penelope's neck.

'Where did you get that?' she asked.

'I found it at home, in the attic,' Penelope mumbled.

'Let me see.' Diana held out her hand and Penelope didn't know what to do.

'Go on, Pen,' Baz said with a grin. 'Give her a gander.'

Having no choice, Penelope gave her mother the opal. Bruce and Baz were overjoyed to see it change hands.

'You can have it back when you learn some manners,' said Diana.

Little Baz looked up at the beautiful lady who now held the opal.

'With the opal in your hand, your every wish is our command,' he said sweetly.

Diana smiled at him in delight. 'How quaint,' she murmured. Bruce's clear blue eyes searched her face.

'If there's anything we can do for your ladyship. Any way we can be of service . . .'

'What a crawler,' Penelope muttered.

'Oh, Bruce,' Diana said smiling at him. 'If wishes came true I'd wish for a hot soothing bath.'

Bruce smiled back and swatted. The filthy bathroom was now sparkling, and the gleaming bath was full of clean, hot water.

Mossie appeared laden with fresh towels and soap.

'Thank you, Mossie,' cried Diana. 'What a wonderful surprise.'

Mossop shrugged. She couldn't explain it, but it was nice to be thanked. Looking forward to a good long soak, Diana kicked off her shoes and handed the opal to Mossop.

'Mind this for me, Mossie,' she said. 'Penelope can have it back when you think she's learned her lesson.'

Mossop headed for the kitchen. Baz smiled up at her.

'You've got the opal in your hand . . .' he chanted. Then his voice faded as Penelope clapped her hand over his mouth.

'Bless his heart,' Mossop said, smiling warmly. 'What the young do come up with.'

In the kitchen, Penelope tried out her best behaviour and her most charming manner as she begged Mossie to give her the opal.

'Please, Mossie. I love you and I'll be sweet forever,' she

implored. Bruce and Baz were almost sickened by her sickly sweet performance, but Mossop finally softened. The genies cursed their luck as Mossop began searching through her pockets for the opal.

'Such a fuss,' Mossop grumbled. 'I wish you'd left the wretched thing where you found it.'

'No!' screamed Penelope, but it was too late. Bruce swatted and the opal flew through the air, all the way back to England and the attic at Townes Hall.

Bruce and Baz gazed happily at the great Australian outback. They were back home, in the land they loved. And best of all, with the opal back in England, they were on holiday with no master.

'I'll get it back,' Penelope informed them with a scowl. 'I'll phone England and have it sent over and then we'll see who's sorry.'

The genies grinned and Penelope marched towards the house. Then she stopped dead. A terrible thought had just occurred to her.

'There's no phone, is there?' she asked.

'Yes, there is,' Baz told her helpfully. 'It's about fifty miles down the road. You can't miss it.'

'Don't be sad,' Baz said sincerely as he tried to comfort her. 'We can still be friends.'

But friendship wasn't what Penelope wanted.

'I'm stuck here,' she wailed.

Then she noticed a strange vehicle approaching. Trailing a cloud of dust, a dilapidated bus pulled up at Townes

Downs. On the side of it were painted the words 'Von Meister Tours'. Bruce and Baz exchanged concerned looks.

The bus was full of tourists. Penelope quickly noticed a teenage boy, who seemed to be the driver's assistant. He was masculine and muscular with long dark hair. In her opinion he was drop dead gorgeous. And, best of all, he carried a mobile phone.

The bus driver had sweat stains on his shirt and grease stains on his shorts. He ambled over.

'I'm Otto Von Meister of Von Meister tours,' he said, extending a filthy hand to Bruce. Bruce's eyes narrowed.

Penelope eyed up the tall dark boy. *He's simply divine*, she breathed to herself. His name was Conrad.

Seven Russian tourists staggered off the bus.

'Okay,' called a young Aboriginal woman who'd also climbed out of the bus. 'Anyone want to use the toilet?'

The tourists rushed towards the house. Diana looked aghast as Otto unfurled a roll of toilet paper. The tourists fell upon it as if it was manna from heaven.

Penelope sidled up to Conrad, who looked her up and down. She looked every inch an English girl in her thick winter clothing.

'Expecting a cold snap?' he asked.

'I came away in a hurry and I didn't pack any summer clothes,' she explained.

She looked at him thoughtfully. He may have been gorgeous, but right now his best feature was his mobile phone.

'Actually,' she said, 'All our clothes are still in England. I was wondering if I might use your phone to ring home for a change of clothes.'

26

Conrad stared at her. He thought all Poms were mad but this one took the cake.

'I'll have to charge you,' he said.

'Of course,' she replied, imitating her mother's graciousness. 'Would I be able to pay you when my clothes arrive? You see, I left my purse in my other clothes.'

Conrad looked at her strangely. 'Came away in a hurry, did you?'

'Rather!' said Penelope snatching his mobile phone. 'What's the code to England?'

Diana tried to keep her distance from Otto, but he kept edging towards her. His smell even put the flies off.

'I always conclude my unique outback experience tours with a night at Townes Downs,' he explained, in what he thought was a smooth charming voice. 'It's the climax of the whole adventure, and it's always been deserted until now,' Otto went on in a wheedling manner. 'Is it all right if we carry on?'

'Oh yes. Do carry on,' Diana replied graciously. She was merely being polite, but Otto was too much of an oaf to realise that.

While Conrad timed the phone call, Penelope asked a removalist in Wiltshire to go to Townes Hall and pack and send summer clothes for herself, her mother and Mossop.

'Also,' she said, 'In a trunk in the attic there's a glass vase, with a black opal in it. Can you make sure that it gets packed too. It's quite priceless.'

Conrad's eyes lit up and he began to look at her with more interest. Penelope squirmed uncomfortably.

'It's not worth anything really,' she said. 'It's more of a lucky charm.'

Penelope didn't realise it, but Conrad knew exactly who she was – the great-great-great-grand-daughter of Sir Claude Townes, the sworn enemy of his own ancestor, Hans Von Meister.

He told his uncle Otto about the opal as they pitched tents at the campsite.

'Townes stole your great-great-grandfather's opal, you know,' fumed Otto. 'We should have owned this land, not them. That black opal was our lucky charm. It's their fault we have to work like slaves.'

'It's their fault *some* of us have to work like slaves,' muttered Conrad. He was doing all the work while his uncle watched.

'We have to get the Von Meister opal back,' declared Otto.

On the other side of the bus Barry and Baz shuddered.

'Hans Von Meister was the worst master we ever had,' murmured Bruce. 'Worse than kids on red cordial.'

'I'm scared, Dad,' Baz said nervously. He had bad memories of being bossed about by Hans Von Meister. He was sure that Otto was no better.

'Don't be scared,' his father reassured him.

'But what if they get the opal!'

'We just can't let that happen,' Bruce said, giving Baz a reassuring wink.

That evening Otto invited everyone to a barbecue at the campsite.

'I don't trust a man who doesn't buy deodorant,' Mossop said firmly.

Diana agreed with her, but she had other things on her mind. She liked the flat open countryside of Townes Downs. There were no paying guests, no nosy neighbours, and no-one who knew of her humiliation back home. She thought briefly of the bumbling Bubbles and was glad he was far away on the other side of the world.

Penelope was aware of her mother's feelings. She was also aware of her own. Her heart thumped as she looked at Conrad. He gave her a cheesy smile and Baz, who was sticking by her side, almost threw up.

'I was only joking about charging you for that phone call,' Conrad told Penelope, trying to sound sincere.

'Thank you. I appreciate that,' Penelope replied, hoping he couldn't hear the pitiful thumping of her heart.

'No wuzzers,' he replied.

Penelope wondered what on earth he meant.

'No probs,' he added cheerfully. She wondered why Australians couldn't speak English. 'I've been trying to work out how old you are.'

Penelope lifted her head and tried to sound sophisticated. 'I don't think it really matters how old you are. I think maturity is more important.'

Conrad took a bite of burnt sausage. 'I told my uncle you'd be about eighteen.'

Penelope was thrilled and flattered. Baz goggled at Conrad's obvious bulldust.

'I'm not quite eighteen yet,' Penelope trilled. 'How old are you?'

'Sixteen,' he replied.

'Isn't that amazing. So am I.'

Baz's jaw dropped at Penelope's blatant lie.

'Has anyone ever told you how beautiful you are?' Conrad muttered. He leaned in closer to Penelope and she closed her eyes, ready for her first kiss.

'G'day Pen,' Bruce cried, appearing from behind a tree. Penelope glared at him and Conrad jumped, knocking his plate full of food into Penelope's lap. His phone rang and he leaped again, this time to answer it.

In the living room of the Townes Downs homestead, Penelope threw a full-scale tantrum.

'You were spying on me,' she roared.

'I was worried. He's just conning you,' Bruce said. 'You can't *trust* that kid. He's just after you for the opal.'

'Trust!' bellowed Penelope. 'You telling me about trust? That's very funny!'

'You don't know the Von Meisters like I do,' Bruce said urgently. 'They're cunning and ruthless and *bad*.'

'When I want your opinion I'll ask for it,' Penelope told him haughtily and stomped out into the hall. Conrad suddenly appeared at the front door.

'There's a message for you,' he said. 'The removalists said your luggage will get here on a freight plane on Wednesday morning at eight o'clock.'

'Thank you Conrad! That's wonderful! I can't wait to ... put on some summer clothes.'

'I can't believe you've fallen for him,' said Bruce, shaking his head as Conrad left.

'Don't be ridiculous. We're just good friends, that's all,' Penelope snapped. Her personal feelings were her own business. It was time to put Bruce in his place and remind him who was boss.

'The opal will be here soon,' she said sweetly. 'So you'd better make the most of your freedom while you can!'

As the sun rose at six o'clock on Wednesday morning, Bruce and Baz heard the drone of a small plane. Then they saw it approaching across the pink and golden sky.

'What's that, Dad?' Baz asked.

'That's the end of our freedom, son. That's Penelope's plane.'

'It's two hours early!'

'Yep. I reckon we better do something about that.'

Baz rushed towards the house as Bruce headed off towards the airstrip. In his haste, Baz didn't think of going through the front door. Instead he flew straight through Penelope's bedroom wall.

'Penelope, wake up!' he cried as he shook her urgently. 'The plane's arrived. With the opal!'

Penelope groggily checked her little travelling alarm

clock. 'It's too early,' she muttered.

'Come on,' urged Baz. 'Before they get the opal.'

'Before *who* gets the opal?' Penelope asked, but she leapt out of bed knowing she couldn't risk it falling into anyone else's hands. Baz dashed out through the door. Penelope followed him. Forgetting in her sleepy state that she had to open the door first, she crashed into it.

'Mossop!' she wailed.

'What is it?' Mossop called from her room.

'I'm locked in!' Penelope cried in despair.

Mossop climbed out of bed and lumbered towards her bedroom door, only to find that she, too, had been locked in. As Bruce helped the pilot unload the freight from the plane, Otto's bus roared towards the airstrip. Baz knew they had no time to waste. He helped first Penelope and then Mossop climb out through their bedroom windows.

'Who could have locked us in?' Penelope asked, bewildered.

'Someone who wants to steal my summer frocks,' Mossop replied darkly.

Diana was quietly enjoying an early morning walk. She felt a peace and freedom she'd never known in England as she watched the colours of the sunrise on the huge horizon. *I love it here,* she thought.

Then her peace of mind was shattered by the sight of Penelope and Mossop running across the plains to the airstrip.

Mossop wasn't surprised, when she arrived out of breath

at the airstrip, to find Bruce and Baz already there. But she was shocked to see that Otto and Conrad had also turned up. They were ransacking the trunks that had arrived from Townes Hall. Her big white bloomers and large bras were scattered around the tarmac.

'Unhand my underwear!' she screamed at Otto.

'You said eight o'clock!' Penelope accused Conrad bitterly.

Mossop frantically tried to collect her clothes from the tarmac, while Penelope desperately searched amongst the scattered possessions for the opal. Unfortunately Conrad came across the glass vase and saw the black opal inside it. Penelope, Otto and Conrad all dived towards it and there was an ugly scuffle before Conrad emerged holding the opal triumphantly.

'We're rich. It's ours again at last!' cried Otto.

'Give it back,' demanded Penelope. 'It's mine.'

Diana crossly stepped up to Conrad and snatched the opal out of his hand.

'Penelope's pendant! What on earth is going on?' she asked.

Everyone began to shout at once. Baz sidled up to Diana and gave her a sweet smile.

'You've got the opal in your hand. Your every wish is our command,' he said.

'It's yours now, Diana,' Bruce added warmly. 'You may as well keep it.'

Diana looked at everyone as if they had all gone crazy and gave the pendant back to Penelope.

'All this fuss over a simple piece of jewellery,' she muttered.

Chapter Three

Penelope wanted to go home to England. Conrad had hurt her badly.

How could he toy with my emotions like that? she wondered. Her mother was so happy, planting a garden in the bare red earth. But Penelope wanted to go away from Australia forever.

Bruce and Baz made plans of their own while they painted Penelope's bedroom floor. Diana had given Bruce a job as handyman and gardener, but Penelope refused to let them do magic to make the work easier. Instead they had to do chores the slow, human way.

'Son,' said Bruce. 'We're going to break free of this slavery. We're going to be masters of our own destiny.'

'Yeah, let's do it, Dad,' Baz cried enthusiastically.

'First, we've got to get Penelope to the cave where the opal was found,' Bruce explained. 'Then we have to get her to wish herself into the opal. And then finally we can wish for our own freedom!'

Baz thought that was simple enough, but Bruce wasn't so sure.

'What are you doing, Baz?' asked Penelope, appearing in the doorway. 'You've painted yourself into a corner.'

Baz looked around. Sure enough he'd ended up in a corner surrounded by wet paint. He gazed up at Penelope, wishing they could be friends.

'How's Conrad?' he asked.

'Conrad?' cried Penelope airily, desperately trying to hide her feelings. 'He's a thing of the past. I got over him ages ago.'

34

'Really,' said Bruce with a grin, gesturing to the great outdoors. 'You know he's been over there spying on you all morning.'

Penelope rushed to the window. In her haste she tripped and fell, ending up with paint all over her clothes and her face. Bruce chuckled.

'Oh, Pen,' Baz said sadly. 'I just finished painting that.'

'I think I'd like to be alone now,' she announced in an aloof voice. But Baz persisted with his friendliness.

'Do you want to come and see our cave?' he asked eagerly.

'What cave is that?' she asked.

'Just a cave we know about,' said Bruce casually. 'But you want to be alone, so we'll see you later.'

Bruce made it sound so unimportant that Penelope was instantly suspicious. Had Baz let something slip? Was the cave important?

A little while later Penelope set off with Bruce and Baz to see the cave. Although she now had her summer clothes, it was hot work crossing the relentless outback country.

A little distance behind them, Conrad, armed with his binoculars and mobile phone, sneaked along and hid behind one skinny gum tree after another. When the trees ran out he hid behind salt bushes. When they ran out, he uprooted the last bush and held it in front of him as he travelled low to the ground.

'If that creep wasn't following us, I could just wish us into the cave,' Penelope muttered tossing her hair. Then another thought occurred to her.

Behind his bush, Conrad was sure he was getting heat-stroke. Ahead of him he saw a tropical oasis, complete with an ice-blue swimming pool and palm trees.

His jaw dropped when he saw Bruce and Baz lounging in deckchairs, sipping fruit cocktails. He gaped with amazement as Penelope smiled and waved to him before diving into the cool refreshing pool.

'Yee haa, bombs away!' he cried as he raced towards them, jumped high and dived into the pool.

Penelope, Bruce and Baz turned away leaving Conrad buried in the sand, his legs waving pathetically.

'Revenge is so refreshing,' Penelope said sweetly.

'Hey Pen, while Conrad isn't watching, why don't you wish us into the opal?' Baz suggested.

'Hang on, son,' Bruce broke in quickly. Penelope looked at him suspiciously. Baz's idea seemed like a good one. Why was Bruce objecting?

'If you wish us into the opal right now, we won't have to walk any further,' Baz said eagerly.

'But . . .' broke in Bruce urgently.

'That's definitely my wish,' Penelope quickly interrupted.

'No, don't,' Bruce cried but it was too late. Baz had already swatted.

Penelope looked around, stunned. She had no idea where she was. This place, with its many colours, looked like no place on earth. The walls had glowing patches of green and red and blue and purple.

'I did it, Dad,' Baz said proudly.

'You certainly did,' Bruce agreed, but he didn't look too thrilled.

'Where are we?' Penelope asked nervously.

'We're inside the opal,' Baz announced excitedly.

'Where's the opal?' Penelope asked, not understanding.

'You're inside it,' Bruce told her flatly. 'You can't bring the opal inside itself unless you're in the cave where it was originally found.'

This was too much for Penelope to follow. But Baz's happy smile faded, and he looked miserable.

'So we should have gone to the cave first,' he mumbled. Being a junior genie was tough. There were so many rules to learn.

Penelope thought things through. 'So we're inside the opal. And I'm not wearing it any more. So . . . if I don't have the opal I can't make any wishes.'

Bruce nodded.

'Where's the door?' Penelope asked, trying not to panic. 'Please don't tell me there's no door.'

No-one told her, but looking around she could see quite clearly that there wasn't one.

'We're only stuck in here until someone holding the opal wishes you out,' Bruce informed her.

'What if no-one finds the opal?' Penelope shrieked. Then she was struck by an equally depressing thought. 'What if it's found but no-one wishes me out?'

Conrad, alone in the outback, talked to his uncle Otto on his mobile phone.

'Of course I imagined the oasis,' he said crossly. 'But they definitely disappeared.'

'Listen to me, Conrad,' Otto's voice echoed down the phone. 'You're just sunstruck. Get a grip on yourself.'

As Conrad listened to Otto he saw the opal, lying in a sandy footprint and glinting in the sun.

'Help!' screamed Penelope inside the opal.

'No-one can hear you scream inside here,' Baz told her.

'It's like a prison,' Penelope moaned. 'There's no kitchen, no toilet, no TV. I'll go mad . . .'

'You won't need a kitchen or a toilet,' Baz told her matter-of-factly. 'Because there's no food in here.'

As Penelope succumbed to utter despair, Bruce began to feel something. His ears began to feel warm, and then they began to burn. He knew that meant a new master. Leaving Baz with Penelope, he disappeared.

Conrad was still on the phone as he rubbed dirt off the opal. Greedily eyeing its blue, green and gold glitter, he asked Otto to come and pick him up. A whiff of dust billowed up into his nose. As he sneezed, Bruce quietly materialised behind him.

'You've got the opal in your hand, your every wish is my command,' Bruce muttered softly. He tapped Conrad on the shoulder, and the boy turned and screamed.

'Where did you come from?' Conrad asked.

'Over there,' Bruce replied, gesturing vaguely over the sand dunes.

'Where'd Penelope go?' Conrad asked in confusion.

'She went off to the cave where the opal was found. There's a whole mountain of opals up there.'

Conrad's eyes lit up with greed. Otto, on his end of the phone, heard the conversation and gasped at the thought of all those opals.

'I bet you Penelope's stuffing her pockets full of opals,' Conrad muttered. 'She's so greedy and selfish. If she gets more opals than me . . .'

Bruce smiled. Conrad was taking the bait.

'Don't you wish you were in that cave right now?' he asked conversationally.

'Oh, mate,' cried Conrad. 'I'll tell you what I do wish. I wish I was right there, in Penelope's face, so I could tell her where to get off.'

Bruce found Conrad's wish terribly depressing, but he had no choice. He swatted and Conrad disappeared. The opal fell into the dirt next to Bruce's feet – but, being a genie, he couldn't pick it up.

'What are you doing *here*?' demanded Penelope as Conrad arrived nose to nose with her.

Conrad couldn't think of an explanation. Too many strange things had been happening.

'What are *you* doing here?' he countered. Then he added, 'Where is here?'

'I'd tell you,' Penelope replied meanly. 'But I'm not talking to low-down reptiles this week.'

'She's not talking to me either,' Baz confided to Conrad.

'Do you know where we are?' Conrad asked Baz.

'Sure,' Baz replied with a grin. 'We're inside.'

'Baz, of course I'm talking to you!' Penelope interrupted in a panic in case Baz was about to spill the secret of the opal.

'You said you'd rather rot at the bottom of a sewer than ever talk to me again,' Baz reminded her.

'That was just a turn of phrase,' Penelope said through gritted teeth.

'And then you said I was as dumb as horse's doo,' Baz continued.

'That wasn't anything personal,' Penelope said, smiling sweetly at him, but Baz was pouting.

Conrad couldn't figure out where he was. Carefully he tapped his way around the wall, searching for an exit. Penelope kept her eye on his mobile phone, and when Conrad had his back turned she lunged for it and quickly dialled.

'It's dead,' she said mournfully.

Conrad grabbed the phone and dialled.

'This phone is guaranteed to work anywhere in Australia,' he boasted. When he got no response, he asked plaintively, 'We are in Australia, aren't we?'

Back at Townes Downs, Diana was searching the house and garden.

'Bruce, have you seen Penelope?' she asked worriedly.

'Baz was talking about showing her his special cave,' Bruce replied.

'So you haven't seen Baz either?' Diana asked in concern.

40

Bruce couldn't very well tell Diana that he and Baz had led Penelope out into the harsh, dry countryside, and that he'd left her stranded inside an opal.

'Oh you poor man, you must be frantic,' sighed Diana.

Bruce looked at her guiltily.

'Perhaps we should go and see if they're in that cave?' he suggested.

'What are we waiting for?' Diana asked.

A minute later she and Bruce were in the rickety old ute, with Diana driving at high speed across the country.

Inside the opal, Conrad sidled up to Baz.

'Baz, old mate. Time for us blokes to stick together, hey?' he asked with a fake friendly grin.

'Don't listen to him,' Penelope snapped. 'You know he can't be trusted.'

Conrad decided he'd try a bit of cunning.

'Don't worry about it,' he said to Baz, and added teasingly, 'You probably don't know how to get out anyway.'

'I do so!' retorted Baz.

Penelope's eyes lit up with hope. 'I love you, Baz,' she cried as she threw her arms round him.

'You're very special to me, too,' Conrad said, trying to sound sincere. Penelope thought he just sounded slimy.

Back at the homestead Otto stood next to his jeep talking to Mossop.

'He could be anywhere,' Otto moaned. Secretly he was

41

thinking greedily of the mysterious cave full of opals more than he was of Conrad. 'He said something about a cave full of opals.'

'That's where Bruce and her Ladyship have gone!' exclaimed Mossop.

'I'll follow their tracks,' cried Otto, galvanised into action. As he started up the jeep, Mossop planted herself in the seat beside him.

Diana and Bruce arrived at the spot where Conrad had dropped the opal.

'Anything over there?' Bruce asked.

'No,' she replied. A second later she gave a startled cry. 'Over here, Bruce. It's Penelope's pendant!'

Bruce pretended to be surprised. Diana clasped the pendant with tears in her eyes, then looked around. The countryside was empty as far as she could see.

'I hope Penelope is all right,' she said with tears welling up in her eyes.

'I'm sure she's fine,' Bruce assured her, gazing into her beautiful eyes. 'You've got the opal in your hand, your every wish is my command.'

'Thank you, Bruce,' Diana replied. She liked Bruce but he seemed strange. He certainly said some very odd things.

She couldn't see any sign of Penelope or Baz so she jumped back into the ute to continue the search. Bruce climbed in beside her.

'Don't you wish we were in that cave right now?' he asked.

Diana smiled sadly. 'Bruce, if wishes were pennies I'd be a wealthy woman.'

The ute jolted as Diana pressed on the accelerator. Bruce was flummoxed. It was going to be tricky to get Diana to say the right words. Her next comment totally floored him.

'Poor Penelope, I hope she's all right. She's so defenceless.'

Defenceless isn't the word Bruce would have chosen for Penelope. Right at that moment she was in a huddle with Baz, whispering to him so Conrad wouldn't hear.

'Baz, did you know that I look on you as the little brother I never had.'

'Truly ruly?' Baz asked hopefully. He'd been very lonely locked up in the opal with only his dad to play with, and he would have loved to have Penelope as a big sister.

'I've always wanted to have a sister,' he told her truthfully.

'That's very touching, Baz,' Penelope said softly. 'I think I feel like crying.'

'I feel like spewing,' Conrad said. Penelope and Baz moved further away from him and dropped their voices lower so he couldn't overhear. It wasn't long before Penelope had Baz trusting her fully. He soon told her that Bruce longed to be set free, even though that meant becoming human.

'Gee,' said Penelope, sowing the seed of an idea in Baz's mind. 'Now that I'm stuck in here, I'll never get the chance to show you and your Dad what a kind and sensitive person I really am.'

Conrad edged closer, trying to catch fragments of their

whispered conversation. Penelope instantly dropped her kind and sensitive manner.

'Watch it, slimebag,' she snarled. 'Get back in your hole. This is a private conversation.'

Bruce and Diana had at last come to the foot of a large mountain. Diana was surprised to think that Penelope and Baz could make it this far without transport.

'I wish I was there right now. Don't you?' he asked hopefully for the tenth time.

'Look, Bruce,' she finally said. 'You've got to stop all this wishful thinking. It won't get you anywhere.'

Suddenly the path fell from under Diana's feet, leaving her clinging to the rocky face of the mountain as dirt and stones tumbled down the sheer drop.

'Your Ladyship, hang on,' Bruce called urgently. Quickly he disappeared, then reappeared on the other side of her where he was in a better position to help. Diana couldn't figure out how he'd done that, but she was in a state of shock and didn't ask questions. Bruce extended his arm towards her but he couldn't reach.

'I just wish I could reach you,' he said honestly.

'So do I,' Diana murmured, terrified of falling.

Bruce swatted as if he was brushing off a fly. Then his arm stretched and stretched and stretched. Diana goggled at it, but she assumed that, in her state of fear, she must be hallucinating.

'Grab my hand, your Ladyship,' called Bruce.

Diana made it safely over the broken path and fell into

Bruce's arms. For a moment their eyes met.

'Thank you,' she said. 'Please call me Diana.'

'Baz,' Penelope said inside the opal. 'If you get me out of here, I promise you can stay in Australia forever with as much freedom as you like. I'll never boss you around again and I'll only ask occasionally, very nicely, for the odd favour.'

'Gee,' cried Baz, his eyes shining, 'That sounds too good to be true.'

'Wait. There's more,' Penelope whispered conspiratorially so Conrad wouldn't hear. 'You'll be like a brother to me. And if you set me free, then I'll set your Dad free, if that's what he wants.'

'Okay,' Baz said simply. Penelope threw her arms around him in relief.

'Let's get out of here,' Penelope muttered.

'I just have to concentrate,' Baz told her.

Bruce and Diana stood at the entrance to a cave covered with spectacular Aboriginal art. A vivid seam of opalescent rock cut a brilliant swathe across the rock.

'Penelope! Penelope!' called Diana. Her voice echoed around the rock walls unanswered.

'She's not here,' Diana cried in distress. 'Bruce, where is she? Where's Baz?'

'I don't think they're very far away,' Bruce told her honestly. Now that Diana had the opal and was in the opal cave, all he had to do was get her to wish herself inside the

45

opal. Then he could wish for his own freedom. He decided he had to tell her the truth about Penelope's whereabouts.

'Look, Diana,' he began. 'I have a confession to make. I haven't been one hundred per cent honest with you.'

'Has something happened to Penelope?' Diana cried in alarm.

'No, of course not,' Bruce said reassuringly. Then he added coaxingly. 'If you just hold the opal . . .'

But Diana cut him off. 'I just wish I could hold Penelope in my arms right now,' she cried with heartfelt sincerity.

Bruce banged his head against the rock wall of the cave. So close, but not close enough. Instead of Diana taking the magic opal inside itself, Penelope and Baz appeared in the cave behind them.

'Penelope, darling!' Diana was filled with relief when she spotted her. 'Thank goodness you're all right.'

'Hi, Dad,' Baz greeted his father cheerfully.

'We were that close to freedom,' moaned Bruce.

'Don't worry,' Baz said cheerfully. 'I've worked it all out with Pen.'

'Mummy, you found my opal!' Penelope said, turning on the charm. 'You are a treasure. Thank you so much.'

At that moment Otto staggered into the cave with Mossop.

'Has anyone seen Conrad?' he asked. No one answered him.

Baz took Penelope's hand and whispered to Bruce.

'Don't be sad, Dad. Pen and I made a deal. We're staying in Australia and you can be free if you want.'

Bruce looked at Penelope with disbelief. What he saw in

46

her face didn't encourage optimism.

'I'm sorry, Baz,' Penelope said in her ever so polite, well bred English accent. Then she dropped her bombshell. 'We're going back to England!'

Baz gasped. 'But you said . . .'

Penelope looked at his shocked little face. She knew in her heart that she had betrayed his trust. However, England was her home. She'd had a terrible time in Australia.

'We agreed that I'd set you free if you set me free,' she explained. 'But you didn't set me free. Mummy did.'

There. It was all above board, but Baz looked at her like she was some kind of low-down manipulative liar.

'But . . .' he began.

Before he could get very far, Penelope jumped in by saying firmly, 'I wish we were all back in England right now!'

Chapter Four

Penelope was enjoying being back in England. Bruce and Baz weren't happy about being forced to live away from the hot sunshine and warm land that they loved. They found England cold and wet and miserable. Penelope told them that was just their bad luck.

Baz couldn't look at Penelope without showing the pain of her betrayal in his eyes. But one day he sidled up to her.

'Dad says I have to tell you I'm not angry with you any more,' he muttered. 'He says you're only human and therefore you can't help it.'

Penelope didn't feel flattered. But she was relieved when Baz laid off the reproaches. She decided that Conrad was only human too. She finally relented and let him out of the opal.

Diana and Mossop didn't seem surprised to find themselves suddenly back at Townes Hall, Wiltshire, England. Whatever magic Bruce had done, he'd done cleverly, and they asked no questions. Even Otto and Conrad had arrived, too, as slightly puzzled paying guests.

'Now look,' Otto said to Conrad. 'You have to move in on Penelope. She's got the opal. It's our only chance.'

'She won't fall for it. Besides, I don't even like her,' whined Conrad.

'I've had five wives and I didn't like any of them,' Otto retorted. He couldn't see what liking a girl, or not liking a girl, had to do with it.

'I wish I could trust Conrad,' declared Penelope. 'I wish he was honourable, principled and totally besotted with me.'

'I can do that!' Baz said, eager to do more magic. But Penelope grabbed his hand before he had a chance to swat.

'I think this is a job for your father,' she said sweetly. For this particular job she wanted an expert.

She looked at Bruce keenly. This time he better not try any funny business.

'Okay Romeo, do your stuff,' Otto whispered. Penelope appeared in the hall at the bottom of the stairs.

'Penelope, I've got something to tell you,' Conrad cooed. 'It'll probably come as a shock to you. It just hit me like a bolt from the blue. Suddenly I know that you're the love of my life, my soul mate, my destiny. I never want to leave your side.'

Penelope wasn't shocked. She was thrilled. She puckered up, ready to receive her first kiss, but was suddenly rudely interrupted by a visitor.

They heard a knock on the door. A police detective stood there.

'Good afternoon, madam,' he said as Mossop opened the door. 'My name is Inspector Graves.'

Mossop led Inspector Graves inside.

'I'm looking for a man called Otto Von Meister,' Graves said. 'He's also known as Crocodile Otto. He's wanted for extradition back to Australia to face criminal charges.'

Conrad stepped forward dramatically.

'Whatever my uncle may have done, I'll stand by his side,' he announced. Penelope sighed. Conrad had suddenly become honourable and principled. He left almost immediately to go and find Otto, who'd suddenly disappeared. The Consumer Affairs department in Australia had received numerous complaints about the horrendous conditions suffered by tourists on Otto's tours. Inspector Graves was determined to find him and send him back to face the consequences.

'Mister Meister's outside,' Mossop said, spotting Otto sneaking away. 'He's a fat repulsive oaf. You can't miss him.'

Before Inspector Graves could catch up with him, Conrad raced up to Otto and grabbed his arm. He was determined that his uncle should do the right thing.

'I'll stand by you,' Conrad declared staunchly. 'If you run you'll only look guilty.'

'I am guilty, you idiot,' hissed Otto. He shook himself free from Conrad and ran towards the woods with the detective in hot pursuit. Conrad wanted to follow, but he turned and his eyes met Penelope's. He sighed lovingly. Penelope smiled smugly. She was enjoying this.

Oh well, she thought. *At least I have Conrad right where I want him.*

Unfortunately Conrad, with his new high principles, had other plans. He found his uncle Otto hiding in the woods.

'We've got to go home and clear our good name,' he declared.

'Why?' Otto asked aghast. 'We don't have a good name.'

'Come on, Uncle,' Conrad urged loftily. 'Where's your honour? Where are your principles?'

'Is that a trick question?' Otto asked but Conrad wasn't going to give up. Eventually he persuaded his uncle to go home. Bruce loaded the Von Meister's luggage into the boot of Graves's unmarked police car as Diana politely said goodbye.

'It's awfully brave of you to go home to face the music,' she commented.

'Not really,' Otto replied. 'There are a lot more places to hide out in Australia.'

'Oh,' Diana said. She didn't know what else to say.

Penelope looked sadly at Conrad.

'Can't you stay?' she asked.

'No,' Conrad replied. 'I can't because I love you. And our future depends on me saving the family business.'

As Graves drove off, Conrad called out the window of the car, 'I'll always love you.'

Penelope smiled sadly. She was missing Conrad terribly. Diana and Mossop and Bruce and Baz were all worried about her.

'I wish I was with Conrad right now,' she sighed without thinking.

'No worries,' said Baz, swatting the air.

Realising too late what she'd said, Penelope screamed . . .

If Bruce wasn't so untrustworthy I wouldn't be in this mess, thought Penelope. She ordered Bruce to peel her another grape. The wide brown Australian landscape struck her as depressing. The only good thing about it as far as she was concerned was Conrad. She waved to him longingly.

In the distance, Conrad was uncomfortably aware of her loving gaze.

'Look at that toffee-nosed, snooty, stuck-up Pom,' he said to Otto. 'She makes me sick.'

'I know how you feel, mate,' Otto said. He too found Penelope a dreadful little snob, but there was something important at stake.

'We'll have to bung on the charm or else we won't get anywhere near that opal.'

It was a hot day. Little Baz was fanning her with a large straw fan, and Bruce's large fingers were trying to peel more grapes for her. It was fun, but she decided they'd had enough of a working holiday.

'Okay, time's up,' she announced.

'We've only been here two hours,' Baz complained.

'I want to go back to England,' Penelope said bossily.

'Come on, mate,' Bruce coaxed. 'You're not being fair to this great country.'

Penelope didn't care about that. 'I want to go back to England. And I want five million pounds in cash.'

'Whoa,' Bruce cried. 'Ease up there. Where am I going to get the money from? You can't just add five million to the pot. That'd cause inflation.'

Penelope wasn't moved by his argument, but Bruce continued. 'When you make a wish you have to think about the consequences. You have to be responsible for your wishes. Instant inflation is highly irresponsible, isn't it, son?'

'Right, Dad,' Baz chirped up.

Penelope looked at both of them coldly.

'Instant inflation!' she said scornfully. 'A real genie would never mention such a thing. I just wish you were one.'

Bruce hated this wish. With a disgusted look on his face he swatted and he and Baz were transformed into traditional genies. They wore bright turbans, gold embroidered boleros, baggy satin pants and ridiculous shoes with curling toes. Being a traditional genie, Bruce now had to talk in rhyme.

'You've just asked for a genie proper
  so here we are in all the clobber,
  I hope to you it gives a thrill
  because I feel like such a dill.'

Bruce snapped his fingers and a magic carpet appeared. He and Baz moved closer to Penelope.

'Mate, we've got the paraphernalia,
  What about a grand tour of Australia!'

Penelope was not impressed, but Baz jumped up and down with excitement. He was sure that if they could show Penelope how beautiful Australia was, she'd fall in love with it and want to stay.

'Come on, Pen,' he urged. 'Let's go for a ride. Dad and I will be your guides.'

'And,' Bruce added, 'To give a verdict true, I'll leave the judgement up to you.'

'I wish you would,' retorted Penelope, realising too late that she'd been tricked into saying those words. The next second she screamed as the carpet soared upwards.

'Yaaa hooo!' yelled Baz as they flew into the sky.

'What's that awful pile of tissue paper down on the shore?' Penelope asked with a sour face as the carpet whooshed through the warm blue air.

'Oh, Pen, don't be such a grouse,' Bruce admonished. 'That's the Sydney Opera House.'

Baz thought Penelope might enjoy the ride more if he made it more adventurous. Happily he bounced the carpet up and down.

'The opal!' Penelope screamed. 'I've dropped the opal!'

Below them the opal sped towards Sydney Harbour. Penelope was terrified that she'd lose it forever in the depths of the blue water. What would happen to her then? She held on grimly as the carpet dived towards the water.

'We're going too fast,' she screamed.

As the carpet neared the falling opal, Penelope reached out and grabbed it. Then she closed her eyes.

'Get me back to Mummy immediately,' she said faintly.

'Is that a wish, my little dish?' asked Bruce.

'Yeeesss,' she replied, her teeth chattering.

The carpet came to a stop behind some bushes near Penelope's house and she climbed off it in a temper.

'No more rhymes, no more costumes, no more flying carpets, and that's a wish,' she ordered.

Bruce swatted and the genie costumes turned back into

their normal clothes. As the carpet disappeared, he and Baz fell to the ground.

'Now I want to go back to England,' demanded Penelope. 'And I want *ten* million pounds in cash!'

Bruce started to argue with her but she cut him off.

'I cannot begin to tell you how much I hate you and this whole country. You and everything about this place make me sick,' she stormed. 'There is nothing in this world, not one single thing that can convince me to stay in this hole . . .'

'Penny, how're you doing?' Conrad called with a cheesy grin as he walked towards her.

The snarl on Penelope's face froze and her expression quickly transformed into a mushy smile.

'Conrad, how are you?' she cooed. Then she quickly hissed at Bruce and Baz. 'Get lost.'

'Take a hike,' Conrad added.

'That's a wish,' Penelope smiled sweetly.

Bruce and Baz hiked off towards the horizon as Conrad slicked back his greasy hair and turned on the charm.

'I was thinking, here you are in Australia and you've hardly seen anything,' he said.

He tried to gaze into Penelope's eyes, but the lovesick expression in them made him feel sick. However, he had his orders from Otto, so he ploughed on. 'I thought I'd show you around.'

Penelope's face lit up. England could wait. Conrad wanted to spend time with her – and she hadn't even made it happen by magic! She hung on Conrad's every word, gazing at him dreamily.

'I thought to meself, now what would Pen like to do.

And I thought the footy. Pen'd love that. My shout.'

Penelope hated footy. It was a game for yobbos and Australians as far as she was concerned. She had no idea that by 'shouting' Conrad meant simply that he'd pay for her. She assumed shouting was an Australian custom at the footy, yelling loudly while you picked dead flies out of your meat pies and tomato sauce. Still, in her lovestruck state, it sounded like heaven to her.

Happily she went to the footy with Conrad.

'Is your opal all right? Do you want me to mind it?' Conrad asked as they sat in the middle of a cheering crowd.

'No, it's fine, thank you,' Penelope replied. One of the teams kicked a goal and the crowd went wild. Conrad leapt up with excitement and his food landed on Penelope's lap.

'Enjoying yourself?' he asked, oblivious to the fact that she was covered in food. Penelope grabbed her opal.

'I wish we were back at Townes Downs,' she said.

Conrad was surprised to find himself back at the homestead, but Penelope acted as if nothing out of the ordinary had happened.

'Thank you ever so much, Conrad,' she said politely. 'That was quite an experience.'

'Yeah, right. Glad you enjoyed it,' Conrad muttered in a confused daze. He wandered off to be interrogated by an inquisitive Otto.

'Wish I was clean,' Penelope murmured as she looked at the food down the front of her clothes.

'I can . . .' Baz began saying, but Penelope cut him off.

'Don't even think about it,' she snapped. Too much of Baz's magic went wrong.

56

'But . . .' Baz started again. This time it was Bruce who interrupted.

'Don't you wish he'd pull his head in?' he said to Penelope with a smile.

'That'll shut him up,' Penelope agreed.

Bruce swatted and Baz's neck seemed to disappear and his head sank down to his shoulders.

'That's better,' Penelope said. Then she began giving orders. 'I want to go back to England and I want *fifteen* million pounds in cash.'

'Where do you want me to get the cash from?' Bruce asked. 'A bank? The Royal Mint? Or from somebody's bank account? Technically it's stealing.'

Penelope refused to get dragged into a discussion about it.

'I want to go home,' she said through pursed lips. But immediately there was another distraction. Diana and Mossop noticed Baz's strange condition. Because he was missing his neck, his head poked out through the opening in the front of his shirt.

'Did something happen to you, Baz?' Mossop asked kindly.

'Yeah,' Baz replied. 'Pen made me pull my head in.'

'Don't be silly, Baz,' Penelope said quickly. 'I wish you'd pull your head out.'

She looked meaningfully at Bruce, who swatted. Baz's head popped out.

'That's better,' Mossop said, patting Baz on the head. 'Don't do it again.'

With a tranquil smile, Diana savoured the fresh air.

'Can you hear that?' she asked.

'What?' replied Penelope. 'I can't hear a thing.'

'The calm and the peace, darling,' said Diana. 'Can't you feel it doing you good?'

Penelope pulled a face.

'I haven't heard any traffic for ages,' Diana sighed, ignoring Penelope's scowls.

'No noisy neighbours,' said Bruce. 'Complete and utter tranquillity.'

Suddenly two noisy Holden cars approached, shattering the peace. Inside the cars were seven local women and a little girl, all bearing plates of cakes, biscuits and sausage rolls.

'Hello,' said Diana, greeting the visitors with a gracious smile. 'I'm Diana Townes. How nice of you to call. Would you like a cup of tea?'

The ladies bustled inside. They'd heard that Diana, their new neighbour, was a titled Englishwoman and they couldn't wait to have a stickybeak at her. One woman was clearly in charge and she pushed the little girl forward.

'Little Kylie would like to recite a poem to make you all feel welcome,' she announced.

The little girl immediately started in a monotonous voice.

'Welcome to my country, it's a land of ups and downs
There are mountains, valleys, rivers, swamps,
There are cities, there are towns.
There's kangaroos and emus and parrots coloured bright,
There are crocodiles and sharks and things
That give a nasty bite.'

Penelope rolled her eyes at Bruce. 'I do wish she'd put a sock in it,' she whispered.

Suddenly the little girl stuffed a red sock in her mouth. The local women looked at her, appalled, but Diana merely murmured to Mossop that it must be an Australian custom. Penelope sighed. She had had enough of Australia and Australians.

'Excuse me,' she said politely. 'I need to go to the lavatory.'

'Wait,' called one of the Australian women. 'Whatever you do, lift the seat first, dear.'

Penelope was shocked.

'It's the favourite place for red-back spiders,' the woman explained. Her hat bobbed up and down on her head as she nodded emphatically. 'A cousin of mine from Boggabri sat on one in a toilet.'

'How dreadful,' Penelope murmured. 'Poor spider.'

In the bathroom, Penelope lifted the toilet seat to check there were no spiders. Then she rubbed the opal. Bruce and Baz materialised in the bath.

'Okay,' Penelope stated firmly. 'No more footy, no more ladies. I want Mummy, Mossop and me to be on a plane back to England. And I want *twenty* million pounds sterling, in cash, on arrival at the airport. That's my wish. Is that clear?'

'Crystal clear. No funny business,' replied Bruce. 'But what about the consequences? Where do I get the money?'

'I don't care,' Penelope responded impatiently. 'That's your business. You work it out. You're a genie.'

Bruce shrugged. Penelope recognised the long, lazy smile that turned up the corners of his mouth. But it was too late to wonder why he was smiling. He was already swatting.

Chapter Five

In England, Penelope lined up at the Customs bench with her mother and Mossop. The flight had been uneventful. Penelope was beginning to relax and believe that nothing was going to go wrong.

'Nothing to declare?' asked a glum-looking customs officer.

'That's right. Nothing to declare,' Penelope replied confidently.

The customs officer unfastened the catches on the suitcase and lifted the lid. He gasped. Penelope, Diana and Mossop peered into the suitcase in astonishment and shock. It was full of money, packed to the brim with bundles of fresh, crisp bank notes.

Bruce and Baz, unable to resist the temptation to watch the fun, materialised behind the customs man. Penelope glared at Bruce in white-hot anger, not realising that the genies were invisible to everyone but her.

'Twenty million pounds,' Bruce said, confirming her worst suspicions.

'You creep! You'll pay for this!' Penelope yelled.

The customs officer assumed she was threatening him.

'Look, Miss, let's not have any funny business,' he warned.

'Calm down, darling,' Diana pleaded with Penelope. She had no idea how the money came to be in her daughter's suitcase, but making a scene in public wasn't going to help anything.

'Can't you see what he's doing?' spluttered Penelope.

'He's only doing his job,' Diana told her.

'Thank you, ma'am,' said the customs officer.

Penelope was almost, but not quite, speechless with fury. 'Not him. Bruce!' she cried.

Bruce chuckled. 'They can't see me!'

Penelope's eyes flashed fire at him and she reached for her opal pendant. 'I'll fix you . . .'

'Just a minute,' said the officer. 'Did you purchase that item abroad?'

He reached out his hand and took the opal. 'Opals are bad luck, you know,' he said.

'It looks like your luck's run out, Pen,' Bruce chuckled.

Penelope lunged forward, ready to throttle him, and accidently banged the lid of her suitcase down on the customs officer's fingers. This didn't help matters, and she, her mother and Mossop were bundled off to wait for the police in a high-security room.

Before long the door banged open, and Inspector Graves barged in.

'Currency violation is a serious offence,' he said in his deep gravelly voice. He turned to stare at Penelope eyeball to eyeball. 'It was in your suitcase, Miss?'

'Yes,' Penelope replied. Then she noticed Baz, who had materialised to watch the action.

'Get out of here and leave me alone,' she hissed at him.

'I wish I could, Miss,' Inspector Graves said. 'But there's the consequences . . .'

Penelope had no idea how she was going to get out of this one. The customs officer had the magic opal, so she couldn't make a wish. Diana and Mossop listened in horror as the detective explained the seriousness of the offence.

'Twenty million pounds went missing from the Royal Mint, with these exact serial numbers,' he thundered.

'Don't say anything, Mossie,' Diana murmured. Mossop had opened her mouth to tell Graves that he was a raving loony if he thought they'd stolen money from the mint.

'Don't get involved. They'd never put us in prison,' Diana added.

She was wrong. The cell door clanged shut firmly behind them.

'How did you manage to acquire twenty million pounds from the Royal Mint?' Diana asked Penelope in disbelief. 'It's the worst thing anyone could wish for!'

'And in unused notes!' Mossop chimed in. Perhaps they would have got away with it if the banknotes were untraceable.

'If the newspapers get hold of this, we're finished,' Diana said wretchedly. 'Imagine if it's on TV. There's only one way out . . .'

'We'd have to move to Australia,' Penelope said glumly.

'Don't be flippant,' Diana chided her. 'No, we'll have to hire the best lawyer in the country. Oh, I wish we could talk to somebody.'

'You could talk to me,' Baz said cheerfully, appearing on the other side of the bars. Penelope looked at him and had a sudden inspiration. She went over to the bars and leant down so she was level with Baz.

'You know that miserable man who has the opal?' she asked. Baz nodded. 'Tell him to wish that I could to talk to someone I know.'

Back at Heathrow, Baz joined Bruce, who was busy telling jokes to the customs officer.

'Hey, mister,' Baz cried. 'Can you wish for someone I know to see someone they know?'

'All right. I wish for someone you know to see someone they know,' the man said. He looked puzzled. 'All right, what's the joke?'

'This is like a nightmare,' Diana said. 'What horror can befall us next?'

The bumbling, fumbling Bubbles arrived to visit them in their cell. Diana almost groaned when she saw him. She wondered if she'd ever escape him, but it turned out he'd brought good news.

'Chin up,' he said in a cheery manner. 'I've brought twenty thousand pounds bail money.'

That cheered Diana up. Next it was Penelope's turn.

'That chap, Bruce, persuaded the customs man to give you this, Penelope,' Bubbles burbled as he handed her the opal pendant. 'Thought it might cheer you up.'

'What about the twenty million pounds?' Mossop asked.

'And the bail money we owe Bubbles,' Diana added.

Bubbles beamed at her. 'There are other ways to repay me, Diana my beloved.'

This time Diana did groan. There was no way she wanted to be grateful to Bubbles. Penelope meanwhile was rubbing the opal and fervently making a wish.

'I wish the money was back where it came from and the whole incident was just forgotten.'

At Townes Hall the soft rain drizzled down.

'I know you're in there, Bruce,' Penelope said as she held up the opal. 'And I wish you to come out in ten seconds.'

Penelope strolled happily over to the smelly compost heap and buried the opal in straw swept up from the floor of the stables. Bruce materialised, his face and clothes smeared with compost, and Penelope grinned at him.

She was sure that from now on he'd know that she'd tolerate no more funny business.

Chapter Six

The front lawn outside Townes Hall was set up for a game of croquet. Penelope watched Bruce with a satisfied smile. He was crouching down, his large fingers gripping a tiny pair of nail scissors which he used to clip individual blades of grass.

'Only three acres to go,' he muttered to himself.

Penelope had been deadly serious about punishing him and Baz for the tricks they had played on her. After they finished trimming the rolling green lawns, they had to clean out the chimneys, starting with the one in Penelope's bedroom. Banned from using magic, they had to work the old-fashioned way.

Baz managed to wriggle his way high up into the chimney to dislodge some stubborn soot. Bruce stood in the fireplace, scraping at soot lower down. Suddenly Baz sneezed and a pile of soot came crashing down, covering Bruce from head to foot.

Penelope looked at Bruce's grimy, gritty, blackened face. Only his eyes showed clearly under the muck, but she could tell his face wore a very weary, miserable expression.

'Fabulous,' she said gleefully. 'There's so much work to be done. Blocked sewerage pipes. Mucking out the stables. The list goes on and on.'

Bruce and Baz looked completely and utterly wretched. With her eyes glinting, Penelope looked meaningfully at Bruce.

'Of course,' she said slowly, 'if you promise not to play any more dirty, double-crossing, low-down, conniving tricks on

me, then we could resume a normal working relationship – without the manual labour.'

Penelope didn't know it yet, but it's impossible to crush
the spirit of a genie, especially an Australian one.

'What if we ease up on the dirty double-crossing,' Bruce
countered, 'but still have a few low-down conniving tricks
every now and then?'

'It's all or nothing,' Penelope snapped. 'Take it or leave it.'

Bruce thought about it and decided to leave it.

'I'm sorry, Pen. A genie's got to do what a genie's got to
do. I'm afraid we can't make any promises that we won't be
able to keep.'

Penelope smiled at him thinly. He may have won the
battle, but he was going to lose the war.

'Very well,' she replied through thin lips. 'I wish you to
clean up this mess – with a toothbrush.'

'Attila the Hun was a better master than her,' Bruce
grumbled. 'The Roman slave boats were a pleasant canoe
trip compared to this.'

'Yeah,' groaned Baz.

'We have to get back to Australia so we can be free.'
Bruce said thoughtfully. A plan was beginning to form in
his genie mind. 'Somehow we have to get the opal off
Penelope.'

'How are we going to do that, Dad?' Baz asked. 'We can't
even touch it.'

'We need someone else to carry it for us,' Bruce said with
a smile. He had just the right idiots in mind.

Baz grinned at him and they both threw down their
toothbrushes. A second later they were spotlessly clean, and

a second after that they appeared on the verandah. Conrad and Otto were deep in a private conversation.

'We can't afford to stay here any longer. We've run out of money,' Otto said gruffly. 'But we aren't going back until we get the Von Meister opal. It's a matter of honour.'

'Yeah,' Conrad grunted. 'And once we get that opal I'm going to really enjoy making that snooty, stuck up, toffee-nosed, pompous, Pommy princess suffer.'

'Don't you like Penelope?' Baz asked curiously.

Otto and Conrad jumped when they discovered Bruce and Baz standing behind a pillar. Bruce leaned conspiratorially towards Otto.

'If we could get the opal off Penelope, would you take it back to Australia?' Bruce asked.

'That's the first thing we'd do,' Otto replied.

Bruce looked at Otto carefully. Otto and Conrad had no idea the opal was magic. He was sure they were stupid enough, and greedy enough, to be lured into the opal cave once they returned to Australia. And then he and Baz could wish themselves free!

'We want to get that opal back to Australia too,' Bruce said. 'But the trouble is that we can't touch it. We're allergic to opals.'

'We can hold it for you,' Otto replied, casting a sly look in Conrad's direction.

'But how are we gonna get it off Princess Penelope?' Conrad asked.

'I have a plan,' Bruce whispered.

Shortly afterwards Bruce and Baz were standing high on a scaffold, painting the greenhouse with whitewash. This was one of the jobs Penelope had given them to do. She had no idea that Bruce had planned a surprise for her. When she walked underneath the scaffold he planned to kick the bucket of whitewash over her. Then Otto and Conrad would grab the opal.

Baz and Bruce whistled cheerfully as they worked. Hearing someone coming, Bruce got ready to shove the bucket with his foot, but it turned out to be Bubbles.

'Ah, Bruce, there you are,' Bubbles called in his tally-ho-old-chap accent.

'Mate, we're a bit busy at the moment,' Bruce said. But nothing was going to put the Pommy prat off. Bubbles climbed up the scaffolding.

'I was wondering if we might have a chat, chap to chap, so to speak, about women,' Bubbles began.

Oblivious to the fact that he was in the way, Bubbles stood on the scaffold between Bruce and the bucket.

'I still carry a torch for Diana,' he said mournfully. 'But she doesn't seem to notice me.'

'Maybe you should carry a neon sign instead of a torch,' Baz commented helpfully.

Bubbles tried to fathom what the boy meant. He never could understand Australian accents.

'I was thinking of buying her an opal,' Bubbles continued. Penelope was so attached to hers that he thought Diana might love one as well, and perhaps some of that love may transfer to him. But he had one problem.

'I've heard opals can be bad luck,' he rambled.

Bruce grimaced. Penelope, Conrad and Otto were right outside the greenhouse, but Bubbles was in the way and he couldn't reach the bucket.

Otto smiled smarmily at Penelope.

'With the greenhouse, I was thinking we should get rid of the plants and put in a genuine solar-heated sauna. What do you think?' he asked.

'Yeah, what do you reckon?' Conrad murmured, trying to look and sound romantic. Penelope smiled at him. Then she glanced up at Bruce and Baz, happy to see them slaving away.

'Keep up the good work,' she called smugly.

'Hello, Penelope,' Bubbles called. Then he accidently kicked the bucket, just as Penelope walked under the scaffold to enter the greenhouse. Whitewash poured all over her and the bucket landed on her head.

She shrieked. Bubbles tut-tutted in dismay, but before anyone had a chance to grab the opal, Mossop appeared.

'Better come up to the house and have a bath,' she advised and led Penelope away.

As Mossop helped Penelope remove her paint-splattered clothes, she noticed splashes of whitewash on the black opal and reached her hand out for it.

'I never take off my opal,' Penelope cried.

'Don't be ridiculous,' Mossop said firmly. 'It's filthy. Give it to me now.'

With extreme reluctance Penelope took the pendant off. She handed it to Mossop, who began rubbing the paint on the surface of the glittering stone.

'Don't rub it too much, Mossie,' Penelope cried. 'Please, please, please Mossie. May I have my opal?'

But Mossop stood firm.

'Look my dear, just for once, I wish you'd do as I ask. I want you clean as a whistle and pretty as a picture.'

Out in the hall outside her bedroom, Bruce swatted. Mossie left the room with Penelope's paint-splattered clothes and the opal. Penelope wailed. It was a strange, high-pitched sound, more like a whistle. In despair she looked at herself in the mirror and saw that her face was flat. It was framed by a large, square, gilt frame.

Otto and Conrad raced after Mossop as she headed towards the laundry with Penelope's clothes.

'Can we give you a hand?' Otto asked eagerly. He tried to grab the clothes out of Mossop's hands.

'Get your hands off these clothes,' she said crossly. 'I do wish you'd keep your hands to yourselves.'

Unseen by Mossop, Bruce swatted and Conrad and Otto found their hands were stuck by their sides. They looked at each other in amazement, but Mossop hadn't finished.

'Get away now, quick smart,' she said shooing them away.

A magic force hurled the Von Meisters twenty feet down the corridor.

'That's more like it,' said a satisfied Mossop. Conrad and Otto looked stunned, but they quickly recovered. They were determined to get hold of that opal one way or another.

Meanwhile, in the large hall downstairs, Bubbles was boring Diana as she walked towards the staircase.

'I know some people say I'm just a rich old bore . . .' he moaned.

'Oh, Bubbles,' said Diana exasperated. 'You're not that old.'

'Exactly,' said Bubbles, not realising what she meant.

At that moment Mossop hurried down the stairs and gave Diana the opal pendant. Behind her Bruce and Baz came sauntering down the stairs, smiling at the whistling noise coming from Penelope's room.

'Here, your Ladyship, you'd better take this,' Mossop said. 'I don't know what's the matter with Penelope. She gets so emotional about this pendant.'

Determined to get her opal back, Penelope came screaming down the stairs in her bathrobe. A large towel covered her square head and flat face. Bruce realised he had to do something fast, or the others would notice and his geniedom would be unveiled. Quickly he turned to Diana.

'As a single parent, don't you wish your child was normal?' he asked.

'I wish that constantly,' Diana agreed.

Bruce swatted and by the time Penelope reached the bottom of the stairs she was back to normal. Suddenly Otto and Conrad ran out from their hiding place. Otto snatched the opal out of Diana's hand.

In the pandemonium that followed, the opal flew backwards and forwards between the Von Meisters. Then they both fled down separate corridors.

'I hate you, Conrad,' Penelope screamed. 'Our relationship is definitely over now. It's finished, do you hear me!'

Whether he did or didn't, Conrad didn't reply.

'Block all exits,' Mossop yelled. 'They're trying to get away.'

Everyone split up and raced along the corridors. Hiding in the scullery, Conrad jumped when he saw Bruce and Baz watching him.

'Where did you come from?' he asked suspiciously.

'Australia,' Baz replied.

Before Conrad could retort, his mobile phone rang. He promptly answered it.

'Von Meister Tours. Can I help you?'

'It's me, you idiot,' hissed his uncle. 'I'm heading for the back door downstairs. I'll meet you there.'

A very tense Conrad peeked out of the scullery and sneaked along the corridor. Beside him strolled Bruce and Baz, both relaxed and happy. They were sure they'd be back in Australia soon.

'Don't you wish we were in Australia now?' Bruce asked conversationally. But before he could reply, Conrad's phone rang again and his uncle told him to hurry up.

Otto had fled up the back stairs to the first floor, certain that no-one would look for him there. Now he crept back along the corridor towards the staircase, but just before he got there Penelope leapt out of a doorway holding a croquet mallet like a weapon.

'Stop, you thief,' she roared. 'Give me back my opal.'

'I haven't got your opal,' Otto cried.

'This is your last warning,' bellowed Bubbles, standing at the other end of the corridor with his own croquet mallet.

'It's not your opal,' Otto sneered at Penelope. 'It's the Von Meister family opal.'

Penelope swung her mallet and a croquet ball went hurtling towards Otto. Bubbles sent another ball flying towards him. Suddenly balls were coming from every direction. Otto's fat tummy jiggled as he tried to side-step them. With a clunk, one ball slammed into his ankle. With a thunk he slipped on another one and went crashing to the ground.

'My bottom,' he moaned. 'I think I've broken my bottom.'

As Penelope and Bubbles raced towards him he dragged himself through a nearby doorway, slammed the door and locked it. A little later, when he peeked out, he found the corridor deserted. He crept along it, clutching his sore bottom, fearful of another ambush.

Conrad made it to the kitchen and crept towards the back door, but Mossop had deliberately spilled oil on the floor. He slipped and slid over the floor and put his hands out to save himself. Unfortunately they landed on the hot plate and he screamed with agony.

'You might as well give up. I don't take any prisoners in my kitchen,' Mossop said, looking at him with slitty eyes as she brandished a frying pan. 'Hand over that opal.'

'I just wish you'd give me a chance to explain,' Conrad said. Bruce and Baz looked at each other disappointed and Baz swatted.

73

'All right,' Mossop said stiffly. 'I'll give you one chance to explain yourself.'

'Big deal,' Conrad said rudely. 'I wish you'd leave me alone.'

Baz pulled a face and swatted.

'All right,' said Mossop. 'I'll leave you alone so you can have a good long think about yourself. You're a disappointment to your family and a disgrace to yourself.'

Conrad was stunned. Mossop, who had appeared so fierce, quietly left the room.

'There you go, mate. Really makes you wish you were back in Australia, hey?' Bruce said eagerly. Conrad gave him a filthy look. He couldn't figure out why this guy and his kid were always popping up.

'Wishing won't get you anywhere,' Conrad replied in a surly voice. 'I wish you'd just shut your mouth.'

Baz swatted and Bruce's mouth shut, although he continued to mumble incoherently about Australia.

As Otto crept down the stairs, Diana, alerted by Penelope, pulled a wire. The rug under Otto's feet went flying and he tumbled down the stairs.

'They're trying to kill me,' he muttered to Conrad on his phone.

'Where are you?' Conrad asked. He'd given up waiting for his uncle and was now creeping around the corridors trying to find him. He pushed open another door.

'Aaaarrrghhh!' Otto replied.

'What?' Conrad exclaimed. 'Speak clearly, I can't understand you.'

On the other side of the door, Otto's phone had been

jammed into his face. With all his strength he pushed the door away.

'Okay, Conrad,' he cried. 'Let's get out of here.'

Bruce mumbled something, but with his mouth shut neither Conrad nor Otto could understand.

'He's trying to say, don't you wish we were all back in Australia now,' Baz translated. Conrad and Otto looked at him blankly.

'No, mate. First we have to sell the family opal,' Otto said. His eyes gleamed at the thought of what it would be worth. So what if this opal was supposed to be the Von Meisters' lucky charm? Otto was sure that money was luckier.

'Don't you wish we were back in Australia?' Baz repeated urgently.

'Tell you what I do wish,' Otto replied. 'I wish we were at a jewellery shop right now.'

Baz and Bruce swatted and in the blink of an eye they found themselves standing with a stunned and confused Otto and Conrad outside a jeweller's shop. Otto and Conrad blinked as they looked around. Basically they had only one thing on their minds. Money! Otto marched into the shop and told the jeweller he had an opal to sell.

'Let me have a look,' the jeweller said thoughtfully. Otto handed over the opal. Baz promptly told him that his every wish was their command. The jeweller, Conrad and Otto all looked at Baz strangely. Conrad was becoming convinced there was something very odd about Bruce and his son.

A deal was soon struck, and Otto and Conrad planned to catch the next flight back to Australia with the money.

'You coming?' Otto asked. Bruce mumbled something that seemed like a no.

'I wish he'd say something,' the jeweller said. Bruce's silence was giving him the spooks.

'Something,' said Bruce obediently, glad he could open his mouth again.

'I thought you couldn't wait to get back to Australia,' Conrad said suspiciously.

'Things were different then,' Bruce replied.

'Here's your half of the money,' Otto said, handing Bruce about only about a quarter of it.

'You can have it. Give it to charity,' Bruce replied.

'Fair enough,' said Otto, planning to give it to his favourite charity – himself. Otto and Conrad scuttled off down the road with their ill-gotten gains.

'There's a lesson in this,' Bruce told Baz in fatherly fashion. 'If you're going to steal something, don't get involved with thieves.'

Bruce and Baz looked with interest at the jeweller. He was looking at them curiously.

'Mate,' said Bruce, turning on the Aussie charm. 'Have you ever thought about taking a trip to Australia?'

'No,' replied the jeweller. 'I don't actually believe that travel broadens the mind.'

Bruce and Baz racked their brains for something to say to make the jeweller change his mind. The jeweller looked at these strange customers and sighed. He often wished his life was simpler.

'I often wish I was a greengrocer,' he told Bruce and Baz. 'You know, selling peas and carrots and aubergines. Ladies would come in and buy my leeks and potatoes.'

Bruce thought all Pommies were potty, but Baz looked at the man keenly.

'Did you wish it just then?' he asked.

'I suppose I did,' the jeweller said. He walked Bruce and Baz to the door of the shop and was astounded to discover a greengrocer's stall had been set up right outside. He looked at the veggies and at the opal in his hand.

'Don't you wish someone would buy that opal for a special lady friend? Bruce asked.

'I do, as a matter of fact,' replied the jeweller. He didn't notice Bruce and Baz swat, but he did see a middle-aged man, carrying a croquet mallet, bumble his way down the road and stop in his doorway.

'I'm not sure why I've come to a greengrocer's,' said Bubbles. 'But I'm looking for an opal for my special lady friend.'

'I just happen to have one opal left,' said the jeweller. 'And I've got some very nice aubergines on special.'

As Bruce, Baz and Bubbles left the shop, Bruce decided it was time to have a man-to-man talk with Bubbles.

'Tell me, mate, have you ever thought of taking a trip to Australia?'

'Certainly not,' replied Bubbles. 'Flies, convicts, sharks, and sheep dung. Just the thought of it makes me ill.'

'Fair enough,' said Bruce with a sigh.

'I've brought you a gift,' Bubbles said to Diana as soon as they arrived back at Townes Hall.

'Oh, Bubbles, you shouldn't have. You're so nice,' exclaimed Diana.

'Unlike those Australians,' Mossop muttered, meaning Otto and Conrad. 'They were here for ages and they left without paying.'

Diana opened the gift and was delighted to find an opal pendant just like Penelope's.

'You've got the opal in your hand, your every wish is our command,' Baz said, smiling up at the beautiful lady.

'It certainly is,' Bruce added sincerely.

'How sweet,' Diana replied. 'I wish we had the Von Meister's money right now.'

Bruce grinned and swatted.

On the plane bound for Australia, Otto plopped his sore bottom down on a cushion and drooled over the money.

'Twenty-five grand,' Conrad chortled.

Otto grinned. Then suddenly he realised something very odd and terrible. The money had vanished.

It was Mossop who found it on the hall table, wrapped up in a piece of paper with the Von Meister letterhead.

'Look at this,' she crowed in delight. 'They paid up *and* they left a tip.'

Everyone was delighted, except for Penelope who had something else on her mind.

'Mummy, you've got my opal back,' she said, thrilled to see it.

78

'Oh no,' Bubbles responded. 'I bought this one from a greengrocer in the city.'

'It's my opal and I want it back!' screamed Penelope. In a panic to get the opal back, she was beginning to throw a tantrum.

'Really, darling, I do wish you'd be more polite,' Diana said softly. Baz wished he had a mother just like her. Even when she was angry Diana didn't raise her voice. Baz swatted and Penelope's attitude instantly changed.

'I'm very sorry that I'm such a naughty and wilful girl,' she simpered. 'I'll try to do better.'

Chapter Seven

There wasn't anything Penelope could do to get her opal back, but she followed her mother around hoping for an opportunity. Bruce and Baz were with Diana nearly all the time, too, granting her wishes cleverly so she didn't suspect they were genies.

Penelope didn't like the fact that Bruce and her mother seemed so friendly. They smiled at each other in a way that made her feel sick. Bubbles also trailed after Diana, hanging on her every word, hoping she'd change her mind and marry him.

'How about a holiday?' he suggested to Diana as they played billiards.

'If you're looking for a holiday, Australia's the place,' Bruce told her.

'The place for heat and dust and flies,' Penelope commented bitterly. 'Snakes and sharks. And the ozone layer has a hole in it.'

Diana ignored the conversation and concentrated on her shot. 'I wish I could clear the table with just one shot,' she commented.

Baz swatted. While Penelope fumed, Diana tapped her cue stick on the white ball. It went whizzing around the table, knocking all the coloured balls into the pockets.

'Good shot,' said Bubbles, astounded.

Baz frowned impatiently. 'So are you going on holiday?' he asked.

'I wouldn't mind,' Diana replied. 'Where do you think we should go, Baz?'

'To the land of no worries,' Baz said with a broad grin.

'That sounds delightful,' Diana said, smiling at the happy little boy.

Penelope became almost frantic with despair but she had to remain polite. 'Please, Mummy,' she began, but everyone ignored her.

'Don't you wish you were there right now?' Baz asked with a twinkle in his eye and a cheeky grin.

'Rather,' said Diana, and there was nothing her daughter could do to stop her. 'That'd be fabulous.'

Bruce and Baz swatted, rapidly and happily, and Diana and Mossop and a sour-faced Penelope were instantly transported to Australia. Alone in the billiard room at Townes Hall, Bubbles looked around and felt dejected. Everyone had gone.

'Look at that flowering cactus, darling,' Diana enthused, pointing out into the baked clay garden at Townes Downs. 'Isn't it amazing?'

Penelope pulled a face. The cactus sucked. Being back at Townes Downs sucked. Everything sucked. And worst of all, here under the hot Australian sun, Bruce and Diana kept gazing at each other with soppy looks on their faces. As soon as Diana and Mossop strolled off down the garden to admire the cactus, Penelope had private words with her ex-genie.

'I want you to stay away from my mother,' she ordered in her bossy voice.

'I can't do that,' Bruce shrugged. He gave her the sort of casual grin that he knew would drive her mad. 'She's the boss. Her every wish is my command.'

'You haven't even told her you're a genie,' Penelope accused.

The smile faded from Bruce's face. He'd been putting off telling Diana the truth.

'You don't want Mummy to know because you're in love with her,' Penelope taunted.

'Oooh aaah,' Baz said. 'Is that why you keep talking to her in your sleep, Dad?'

Bruce tried to deny it, but he couldn't convince either Baz or Penelope.

'I don't want you to be in love with my mother!' Penelope thundered.

Bruce looked her straight in the eye.

'Penelope, love has a mind of its own, and I have a mind of my own too,' he explained. Then he added pointedly, 'And you don't have the opal.'

Penelope screwed up her face, partially because of the harsh sunlight but mostly because she hated the situation.

'I'm going to change into my gardening clothes,' Diana called as she headed for the house. Penelope hurried after her. Sure enough, when Diana changed her clothes and rushed back to the garden she left the opal behind. Penelope quickly filched it.

Taking the opal out on to the veranda, Penelope rubbed it with mad glee and summoned the genies.

'So you stole the opal from your poor mother,' cried Bruce, trying to shame her.

'And who stole it off me in the first place?' Penelope demanded.

Bruce and Baz looked at each other but neither answered. Technically it had been Otto and Conrad, but they kept quiet because of their own involvement. Penelope had them right where she wanted them.

Out on the dirt road the Von Meister bus lurched towards Townes Downs. Penelope spotted the approaching stream of dust and sighed. Despite herself, her heart gave a lurch. She knew that Conrad was a creep who had stolen her opal, but still he was very good looking in a greasy-haired kind of way.

'We can't go back to England right away,' she announced to the genies. 'Because Mummy's bonding with the earth and Conrad will be here soon. However, if you won't fall out of love with Mummy, then Mummy will have to fall in love with someone else.'

'Don't do it, mate. Be sensible,' Bruce said, looking at her with his honest blue eyes. But Penelope wasn't listening.

Otto stepped out of the bus, scratched his belly, hitched up his filthy shorts, then spat in his hand and used it to smooth his hair. Seeing that the Towneses were back in Australia, he had come up with a new plan. He'd turn on his all his charm and get Diana to marry him. That way he'd gain control of Townes Downs and the opal.

He smiled and waved at Diana who was tending the cactus with Mossop. Diana shuddered.

'That man is absolutely repulsive,' she murmured to Mossop.

On the verandah, Penelope, Bruce and Baz watched fat Otto amble towards Diana. Bruce was shocked by the little smile playing on Penelope's lips.

'You wouldn't!' he said shocked.

'It's up to you, Bruce. If you're sensible, it doesn't have to happen.'

'I can't change the way I feel, Pen,' Bruce replied honestly.

'Then I wish for Mummy and Otto to fall in love!' she declared.

'He's revolting,' Diana murmured. Otto scratched his bum as he walked towards them.

'If you shake his hand you feel diseased. If he looks at you, you need a bath,' Mossop muttered as she glared at Otto. 'He's vile, putrid, repellent . . .'

'Oooh, Otto,' Diana suddenly crooned. 'I can't resist you any longer.'

In slow motion Diana and Otto ran towards each other, their hands outstretched. The tourists clambering out of the bus gaped, while Mossop, Bruce and Baz looked horrified. Penelope smiled.

As Diana and Otto kissed, Bruce turned pale and Baz turned green.

'They're sort of eating each other,' he complained. 'It's icky. I think I feel a bit sick.'

Penelope smirked at Bruce. 'Why don't you be sensible and give up?'

'My heart won't let me surrender,' he replied. 'Even though my stomach's not doing too good.'

'Perhaps we need to distract your heart,' Penelope said dryly. 'I see two ladies and I wish they'd both fall in love with you.'

Bruce braced himself and swatted. The middle-aged Mossop smiled at him coyly and Trish, Otto's tour guide assistant, beamed as she walked up to him.

'G'day, mate,' she said as she gazed lovingly at him. 'How's it going?'

'S'going alright,' Bruce mumbled.

'I'll see you later then, hey?' Trish gave Bruce a dazzling smile full of promise and ambled off.

'How romantic,' Penelope commented dryly. 'Is that love Aussie style? I think love should be more poetic. In fact I wish you'd bring out the romantic poet in Conrad.'

'I'm only a genie,' Bruce complained. 'You'd need a surgeon to do something like that.'

Penelope glared at him and Bruce swatted.

Mossop patted her hair, checked herself in the mirror and put some lipstick on. Then she put a record on the old record player.

'Care to dance?' she asked Bruce.

'I thought you'd never ask,' Bruce replied.

Penelope beamed as Conrad walked towards her.

'Our love we will enhance,
 If we pair up for this dance,' he intoned.

Penelope dreamily began dancing with Conrad. She noticed Otto and Diana holding each other so closely they could have crushed his fleas.

'Looks like they're vacuum packed,' she smirked at Bruce.

Conrad grinned. Then he suddenly remembered something he'd left in the bus and ran off.

'Pen, I reckon you should call the whole thing off,' Baz said, holding his stomach. All this romance was so icky he thought he might throw up.

'Don't be ridiculous,' she snapped. 'I'm having too much fun.'

Conrad returned from the bus carrying a grubby box of chocolates which he thrust into Penelope's hands. Then he placed his own grubby hand on his heart.

'The time has come, my love has waited,
  My heart's the hook that you have baited.'

This time Baz was sure he going to throw up, but Penelope giggled and fluttered her eyelashes. Absolutely delighted, she opened the box.

'Soft centres, my favourites,' she cooed.

The centres were soft but so, too, were the outsides. In the heat the chocolates had melted. Penelope popped them in the freezer in the kitchen. A while later she retrieved them and discovered they'd frozen into one big lump. Despondently she dumped the hard chocolate glob down on the kitchen table.

Baz zapped through the wall.

'Pen, you have to change the wish,' he cried breathlessly. 'They're going to get married.'

'Who's the lucky woman?' Penelope asked nonchalantly. 'Mossop or Trish?'

Before Baz could reply, Penelope looked up to see her

mother and Otto standing at the window.

'We've got an announcement,' Diana said excitedly.

'We want you to be the first to know. I want you to call me Dad,' Otto smirked.

Penelope tried to keep a smile on her face, but it was too difficult. She thought she should say something, but she knew if she opened her mouth she'd scream.

'She's speechless,' Otto exclaimed. 'That's how thrilled she is.'

'My lady, don't forget there's nothing wrong with a long engagement,' Mossop cried. 'Ten or twenty years!'

'Oh, no, Mossie,' Diana trilled. 'We're going to tie the knot next week.'

'Our love won't wait,' added Otto.

'Penelope, aren't you going to kiss your new Dad?' Bruce asked, hugely enjoying her discomfort as Otto puckered his slobbery lips.

'I'll wait till the day of the wedding,' Penelope muttered. 'Mummy, are you sure about this? It's all so sudden.'

'Of course I'm sure,' Diana replied. 'Otto and I are going to be together forever. We're going to have lots of children. And we're going to renovate . . .'

Conrad picked that moment to waltz up to Penelope.

'I cannot wait another second,
Tell me what you reckon.
Do you agree our love is blissful?
Is it not obvious in every kissful?'

'Not now, Conrad!' Penelope groaned. She tried pushing him away, but nothing except magic would stop his awful poetry.

'I love you night and day,' he moaned. 'Please don't push me away!'

'Away!' she shrieked. Her nerves had gone to pieces. 'Right now I wish you were on the other side of the world.'

'I can do that!' Baz said quickly, snapping his fingers.

Nobody noticed he'd gone, but Diana quickly realised Otto was missing too. She looked around frantically.

'Have you seen Otto anywhere?' she asked.

'I thought you and he had been stapled together,' Penelope replied rudely.

'What am I going to do?' Diana sobbed. 'I can't live without my Otto.'

Bruce and Baz went looking for him and found him hiding in the bus.

'It's not that I don't love her,' Otto explained, wiping his nose on the back of is hand. 'It's just that she mentioned renovations. I hate renovations!'

Otto's phone rang and he stared at it. He didn't want to talk to anyone, in case it was Diana, but he didn't want to miss out on business if it was a business call. Finally he answered it.

'Crocodile Otto can't take your call at the moment,' he announced. 'Please leave a message after the pip. Peeeeep.'

Freezing at the North Pole, Conrad chipped an icicle off his mobile phone.

'Please pass on this message for me
To my darling Penelope.
Now that we are two apart
Coldness fills my aching heart.'

Conrad shivered and hung up. Otto hung up too and

looked thoughtful. Conrad was clearly insane. It was up to him to do what he could for the Von Meisters.

'What have I been thinking about?' he cried. 'Despite the renovations, I'll beg her to take me back.'

'Dad!!!' cried Baz. There must be some way Bruce could stop this.

'Son,' Bruce said slowly. 'Tell Pen the marriage is on . . .'

'That's it, mate,' Otto said, rubbing his filthy hands together. His eyes lit up with greed. 'We'll get hitched straight away. What's mine will be hers and what's hers will be mine.'

Bruce and Baz looked at each other worriedly and Baz rushed to the house.

'Otto wants to get married straight away,' he cried as he raced into the kitchen.

'Oh gentle love of my life,' Diana crooned. 'I knew he'd come back.'

She swept the white tablecloth off the table, wrapped it around herself and grabbed some half dead flowers from a vase.

Earlier on Bruce had met some of Otto's tourists, and he now made an announcement that made Penelope's eyes go wide with horror.

'We've got a minister here who's ready and willing,' he announced cheerfully. She shuddered. 'What do you say, is this a good day for a wedding, or what?'

Unfortunately, Penelope was shocked speechless. She gathered with Mossop, Baz and the tourists in a small circle as the minister began performing the ceremony. Bruce was best man and he looked meaningfully at Penelope when the minister asked if anyone had any objections. But she couldn't find her voice.

'I object,' Baz piped up. 'It's too icky.'

Finally Penelope's tongue unglued itself from the roof of her mouth. 'I wish everything was back to normal,' she whispered.

Otto and Diana looked at each other. Otto had a mushy expression but Diana looked like she'd just woken up in the middle of a bad dream.

'Don't worry about Baz. We want to get hitched, don't we, darl?' Otto said.

But Diana had changed her mind.

'I feel sick,' she cried.

The marriage was off and Penelope ruefully decided that from now she'd mind her own business. She knew there were some things that people had to sort out for themselves without interference – but she hated the way Bruce and Diana looked at each other. It was icky.

Chapter Eight

After that Penelope was a quieter, more thoughtful girl. She took to spending long periods of time locked away in her bedroom working on her computer.

Finally one day she printed off the last page of a thick document and read it through carefully. Then she rubbed the opal with slow deliberate movements. Bruce and Baz appeared and she handed Bruce the document.

'Here is the perfect wish,' she announced. 'No more accidently misinterpreting what I say. No more twisting my wishes. Everything I want is here in black and white. I want you to read this and weep.'

As Bruce and Baz read the document, fat tears rolled down their cheeks. Penelope had made the perfect wish. This time she was sure she had outsmarted them. As Bruce dried his eyes he gave a miserable swat.

'Here we are back in England,' Bruce declared, wiggling his eyebrows at the suddenly beautiful Penelope.

I'm perfect, Penelope thought smugly to herself. Bruce and Baz had done their job well. She was beautiful, her mother was rich and Mossop was happy, all exactly as she wished.

The living room at Townes Hall had been turned into an office. Diana barked orders down the phone, and Penelope gazed happily at the assistants who counted up the Townes fortune on computers.

'Darling,' announced Diana, taking a moment out of her

91

busy wheeling and dealing. 'Study these brochures. I want to buy you a Pacific island for your birthday.'

The phone rang and Diana picked it up.

'You're the perfect daughter,' she murmured to Penelope before she got back to business.

'I think it's time for you two to find a job, out in the world somewhere,' ordered Penelope.

'But I don't have any qualifications,' Bruce blustered. He didn't want to be sent away from Diana.

'I'm sure you'll find a position somewhere,' Penelope said carelessly. 'In fact, that's a wish.'

'Bye, Pen,' said Baz. Penelope admired her shiny chestnut hair in the mirror.

Downstairs a string of visitors approached Townes Hall and vehicles roared up the gravel drive. As a television crew unpacked their camera equipment from a large van, a big fat blonde woman and a slim, dark-haired girl in a tartan mini-skirt knocked at the front door.

'They're not going to fall for this,' muttered the girl with a surly expression.

'Have you got any other ideas?' hissed the fat blonde woman. 'We have to get that opal.'

The pair were Conrad and Otto in disguise. Having discovered that Penelope and Diana had left Australia and returned to England, Otto had come up with a bold plan to get the opal back again. Conrad was sure it wouldn't work, but when Mossop answered the door any suspicions she may have had were allayed by Penelope's wish that she be happy at all times.

'We booked in for a bed and breakfast two months ago,' Otto told the beaming Mossop.

'I'm happy to say we don't take paying guests any more,' Mossop said, smiling even more happily.

'Please, couldn't we stay one night?' Otto begged.

'Oh, all right,' Mossop agreed, smiling so broadly that her face ached. Behind the two guests she noticed the television crew and shouted up the stairs to let Penelope know they'd arrived.

Doris, the TV producer, appeared to be thrilled to meet Penelope.

'We really want to show the world just how perfect your life is,' she said. 'I think it will be a great inspiration to a lot of people.'

'I certainly hope so,' replied Penelope, not caring if she didn't sound at all modest.

'We're calling the story The First Perfect Person,' Doris announced, much to Penelope's pleasure. Then both of them noticed a white stretch limousine pull up the drive.

'Good, here they are!' Doris announced. 'We've just signed up two new presenters. You'll love them. They just appeared in my office, out of nowhere.'

Penelope had a weird feeling, and a second later her worst fears were realised. Bruce and Baz, resplendent in smart jackets and ties, climbed out of the limo and strolled towards her.

'Bruce! Baz! Good to see you,' cried Doris. 'Meet your first guest – Ms Perfection herself, Penelope Townes. Penelope, meet Bruce and Baz, the stars of the show.'

Stars! Penelope had assumed she'd be the star. She stared at the genies in shock, and they both grinned back.

'Isn't this great!' Baz said ecstatically. 'We've got real jobs.'

In the kitchen, Doris issued instructions to the TV crew as she planned the shoot.

'I think we'll start in here with Mossie.'

Bruce smiled at the housekeeper.

'You'd have the lowdown on Pen, hey?' he asked.

'Oh yes, since she was a baby,' Mossop replied. 'Always an angel. Even when everyone else hated her. Even when she had no friends at school, had bad breath and acne . . .'

Penelope, the perfect girl, looked like she could kill Mossop, who happily burbled on with Bruce's encouragement.

'Then we cut to the loving mother,' Doris decided. 'You know, perfect daughter, perfect mother.'

It seemed like a good plan, but the TV crew found a problem when they entered Diana's busy office.

'Look,' Diana said flatly. 'Time is money and I'm worth four thousand a second, so I don't have time to waste on some cheap, corny TV show. No offence.'

Penelope frowned. She hadn't realised that making Diana rich would change her.

'But Mummy,' she implored. 'You're my mother. I need your motherly support and encouragement and unconditional love to show how perfect my life is!'

Bruce smirked as Diana impatiently checked her watch.

'Do you have to make such long speeches, Penelope?'

Diana snapped. 'Time is money!'

'Look, how about we just duck in here for a quick shot of you at work,' Doris interjected. 'That way you won't lose any time and we'll still get the feeling that you have some interest in Penelope.'

'Two minutes tops,' Diana declared firmly.

'Could we have your autograph?' asked a fat blonde woman. She looked suspiciously familiar, but there wasn't time to ask questions.

The crew was ready to start shooting when the phone rang in the kitchen. Mossop answered it.

'I like it,' Doris muttered. 'It's real.'

She gave the signal and the camera started rolling while Mossop was on the phone. Bruce and Baz turned to the camera.

'No-one knows Penelope better than Ms Mossop,' Bruce announced.

Mossop hung up the phone. 'Good news?' Bruce asked.

'Very happy news!' Mossop laughed. 'My aunt Amy, who raised me since I was five, just dropped dead.'

The TV crew gawped at her as she chuckled. The producer bustled them out. Diana's interview was next, but she frowned at the disruption when the crew entered her office. Baz, with a big grin, turned to the camera.

'How did Penelope get to be so perfect?' he asked. 'We're going to ask her mum, Lady Diana Townes.'

'We want a word of wisdom from the perfect mother,' Bruce added.

'Don't have children,' Diana advised before turning back to her work. 'They bleed you dry.'

'Doesn't Penelope have perfect skin?' the make-up artist commented. She whipped off Penelope's opal pendant before the perfect girl had a chance to make an objection. 'But Penelope's so perfect, I wish she had a few problems, to give me something to do.'

'That was a wish, wasn't it?' Bruce asked Baz.

'I reckon so,' Baz replied with a grin.

Both of them swatted and Penelope began to feel a strange sensation. The camera operator looked up from his viewfinder in disbelief. Penelope suddenly had eyebrows like a werewolf and large pointy ears like a garden gnome.

'Now that's what I call a challenge,' the make-up artist said.

'I like it,' Doris declared. 'It's real. Action!'

The camera started rolling and the cameraman got a great closeup of Penelope, her eyes goggling and her thick bushy eyebrows quivering in misery.

Bruce looked smugly at the camera.

The sound of a scuffle interrupted the interview as Otto and Conrad suddenly tried to wrench the opal from the make-up artist, who clung to it grimly.

'Give it to me, it's mine,' Penelope screamed as the cameras recorded the struggle for the opal.

Bruce and Baz cracked up laughing as they watched the fight. Penelope threw herself at the girl in the tartan skirt who was trying to help the fat woman.

'Get your hands off me,' Conrad yelled.

Penelope realised who he really was and gasped in shock.

Meanwhile the make-up artist grabbed the fat woman's hair and pulled hard. A bushy blonde wig came off in her hands, revealing Otto's filthy curls. The hairdresser tried to help the make-up artist and the film crew got in the way as they moved in for close-up action shots.

Otto managed to grab the opal and Penelope threw herself at him. While the make-up artist and hairdresser sat heavily on him, Penelope prised his fingers open and ripped the opal away from him.

Panting, she turned to Bruce to make a wish. But Bruce was busy.

Looking straight into the camera he cheerfully said, 'So there it is – Penelope's Perfect Life.'

'Some people have all the luck,' Baz added happily.

Penelope scowled.

'There are no words black enough to express how I feel,' she said bleakly after the TV crew had gone and Otto and Conrad had been thrown out. Unfortunately the TV programme had gone to air straight afterwards. Penelope turned the television off when the programme ended, shuddering at how embarrassing it was.

'Look on the bright side,' Bruce urged. 'You're world famous now!'

Penelope winced. Then she thrust the perfect wish document at Bruce.

'I wish you to reverse the perfect wish,' she said bitterly. 'Every last bit of it!'

Chapter Nine

Back at Townes Downs, Penelope wasn't very happy. First, she didn't like being back in Australia, although her mother seemed very happy. Secondly, Bruce and Diana were very friendly and Penelope didn't like that at all. And thirdly, Conrad was paying her no attention at all. Instead he seemed to be playing some sort of spying game with Baz.

She was very surprised one morning when Conrad came to her room for a private talk.

'It's about Bruce,' Conrad announced, knowing that Penelope was hoping it would be something more personal, more romantic.

'Bruce!' Penelope said in surprise.

'Yes. He's not normal,' Conrad cried, screwing up his eyes. 'You think about it. Have you ever seen him eat, drink, wash or attend to any bodily function?'

'No,' replied Penelope. 'But I know there's a perfectly logical explanation. It escapes me right now, but I'm sure there must be one.'

'I reckon he's either a vampire, a ghost or an alien,' Conrad explained.

Penelope looked dumbfounded. Conrad continued. 'He could be a warlock or a humanoid robot like the Terminator.'

'Errr, right,' Penelope gurgled, not knowing what else to say. She goggled at Conrad, who looked defensive.

'Well, he's not normal, is he?' he challenged.

'Bruce *is* normal in his own twisted way,' Penelope insisted.

'No he isn't,' commented Conrad. 'There's something

strange about Bruce. And I'm going to work out what it is. Will you help me or not?'

Penelope, put on the spot, thought fast. It was best if she went along with Conrad's scheme so she could keep an eye on him and hinder him where necessary.

'Of course I'll help you,' she murmured.

'It's going to be very tricky,' Conrad told her. 'I've got Baz watching him now.'

'You've got Baz spying on his own father!' Penelope exclaimed.

'He thinks it's a game,' Conrad replied smugly. 'I've got a feeling Baz'll be able to give me some valuable inside information.'

Down by the dam, Penelope found Bruce and Baz inspecting the pump. It was broken, but Bruce magically fixed it so Diana could water her beloved garden.

'We're in trouble,' Penelope wailed. 'Conrad suspects you're not human. He's spying on you.'

Bruce wasn't at all bothered. In fact he smirked at her distress.

'Don't worry, we know,' he chortled. 'Baz has been spying on Conrad.'

'I'm a double agent,' Baz explained with a cheeky grin.

'If Conrad finds out that you're genies he'll stop at nothing to get you in his power!' Penelope warned. 'He's already pumping Baz for information.'

'All part of our plan,' Bruce said casually.

'We're confusing him with the truth,' Baz laughed.

'The truth!!!' Penelope cried in alarm.

'Relax,' Bruce said as he saw her turning purple. 'We're

not going to tell him what we are. A genie only reveals that to his master.'

But Penelope couldn't relax. Pretending to help Conrad with his plan to trap Bruce, Penelope went with him to see Mossop in the kitchen.

'Let me do the talking,' Penelope whispered. Conrad agreed, but he pulled a face. He hated it when Penelope was bossy.

'Mossie, we're really worried about Bruce,' Penelope explained.

'We've never seen him eat,' Conrad added.

'Of course not,' Mossop replied matter of factly. 'He doesn't eat with us.'

'We know that, Mossie,' Penelope said. 'But Conrad has been watching him closely and he thinks he *never* eats.'

'He looks very strong for someone who's starving,' Mossop observed.

'Sure, he looks healthy,' Conrad suggested. 'But maybe it's just a cover-up. Maybe he has anorexia nervosa.'

'How are we going to feel when he collapses and dies of starvation, leaving poor Baz a homeless waif?' Penelope wailed dramatically.

Mossop looked concerned. She was very soft hearted, and although Bruce looked as strong as an ox, if Penelope was worried she'd do what she could.

'I'll bake him a shepherd's pie,' she promised.

Penelope was convinced that once Conrad saw Bruce eating, he'd give up his theory that Bruce wasn't human. However, Bruce and Baz had a problem with the plan.

'But genies *don't* eat,' Bruce explained.

'We don't eat because we don't,' Baz added, trying to help in his tangled way.

'Everyone has been invited to eat lunch – and if you don't eat Conrad is going to be suspicious,' Penelope said firmly. 'So you have to make it look like you're eating.'

'But . . .' Bruce began.

'But nothing,' Penelope interrupted. 'That's a wish.'

During lunch, Conrad kept his eyes glued on Bruce.

'Hey,' shouted Baz, demanding everyone's attention. 'What do you get if you cross an elephant with a kangaroo?'

No-one knew the answer.

'Big holes all over Australia,' Baz said, screaming with mirth.

During the distraction Bruce zapped his slice of shepherd's pie onto Otto's plate. The fat man looked at it in surprise, then greedily started eating it.

'More pie, Bruce?' Mossop asked.

'Thank you,' Bruce replied, enjoying the look of astonishment on Conrad's face when the boy realised his plate was empty. Conrad stared at Bruce suspiciously. While his attention was diverted, Baz zapped his own pie onto Conrad's plate.

'Aren't you eating, Conrad?' Diana asked.

'Of course I am,' Conrad replied. Then he leapt back when he realised his plate was full. He knew he'd eaten every mouthful of his pie. He squinted thoughtfully at Bruce.

'I didn't see you eat that pie,' he stated meaningfully.

Bruce pointed at the slice of pie that Mossop had just served him.

'I haven't eaten this pie yet,' he pointed out reasonably.

'The pie before,' Conrad specified.

'I didn't know you were watching,' Bruce commented casually.

'I'm not,' Conrad replied.

'Oh well, that's why you didn't see me eat it,' Bruce said pointedly.

Bruce enjoyed teasing Conrad. Penelope wished he would restrain himself as she noticed Conrad getting more and more angry.

'I know what you're up to,' Conrad said huffily. 'You're trying to make me look silly.'

Bruce didn't think Conrad needed any help at all to look silly. He looked at Conrad calmly as the boy reached across the table and accidently on purpose spilled gravy all over him.

'I'm sorry,' Conrad said, not sounding like he meant it. 'I'll help you clean up.'

'Thank you,' Bruce replied. 'But I can wash myself.'

'I insist on cleaning you up,' Conrad muttered through clenched teeth.

'Thank you for your support and encouragement,' Bruce said humorously, as everyone began to stare at Conrad. 'But I can wash myself.'

'May I go with you?' Conrad asked determinedly.

'To the bathroom? I usually go by myself.'

'Will you be using water?' Conrad asked as everyone gawped at him.

'I'll have to make that decision when the time comes,' Bruce said casually. He left the table and ambled towards the bathroom. Realising that everyone was staring at him, Conrad blushed scarlet and Otto glared at him.

After lunch Otto dragged Conrad out to the bus and had cross words with him.

'How will acting insane help us get the opal?' he asked the scowling Conrad.

'Listen to me, Otto,' Conrad replied. 'I'm onto something much bigger than the opal.'

'What?' Otto asked, rolling his eyes as if Conrad had a kangaroo loose in the top paddock.

'I can't tell you,' Conrad shouted and stormed off.

As Diana and Bruce pottered about the garden after lunch, Conrad and Penelope spied on them from under the house. They hid behind the old wooden pilings that held up the rickety building. Baz peeped out from behind another wooden pillar. He was happily spying on Conrad and Penelope.

'I'm thinking of planting flowers here,' Diana said as Bruce installed a sprinkler system. 'And perhaps a peach tree over there.'

Suddenly Conrad and Penelope sprang at Bruce. Conrad thrust a bunch of garlic in his face and Penelope, hanging back a little, hovered with a jar of crushed garlic. According to Conrad, it was a well-known fact that vampires were afraid of the strong smelling substance.

'Scared of garlic?' sneered Conrad.

'Not really scared,' Bruce replied. 'It just gives me gas.'

Diana looked at Conrad as if he'd lost his mind. In an embarrassed huff, Conrad walked off, followed by Penelope.

'I feel so stupid,' he said. 'Of course he's not a vampire.'

Penelope began to relax.

'He wouldn't be out in the sun if he was a vampire,' Conrad pointed out and Penelope sighed. The danger wasn't over yet.

A short time later, Conrad sneaked off to the dam with his video camera. Baz darted out from behind a tree and sneaked along after him.

'What are you doing?' Penelope asked. Baz jumped. He hadn't realised Penelope had sneaked up on him.

'I'm a double agent,' Baz announced proudly.

'You know what's even better than being a double agent?' Penelope asked.

'What?' asked Baz.

'A *triple* agent!' Penelope told the little boy.

'Wow!' cried Baz, his eyes shining at the thought of it. 'A triple agent! I can do that!'

'Right,' said Penelope crisply getting down to business. 'You keep spying on Conrad for your Dad, and on your Dad for Conrad. But you're really working for me.'

Baz happily nodded. Being a triple agent sounded like triple fun.

'Now listen carefully,' Penelope said in her poshest voice. It was important that Baz get this exactly right.

'Conrad has gone to the dam to catch your dad doing something weird on camera. Your mission is to get there first and warn him. No genie stuff. No magic. Just act normal. Show up on film. And don't disappear.'

'Right,' said Baz. He zapped off to the dam and tried to remember what Penelope had told him.

'You have to disappear on film,' he told his father.

'She said that?' Bruce asked looking puzzled.

'Yeah,' Baz said and added importantly. 'I'm a triple agent.'

Conrad set up his camera, knowing that if Bruce was really a ghost he wouldn't show up on film. He glanced up from the camera and stared hard at the dam. Although Bruce and Baz had been there a second ago they'd disappeared without a trace. Conrad spent some time searching but he couldn't find any footprints.

As Conrad raced back to the house with his camera, Penelope intercepted him.

'Conrad, why don't you give this a break?' she asked. 'You're stressed out. You're obsessed.'

'Of course I am,' Conrad agreed. But nothing was going to stop him from trying to photograph Bruce.

'Okay,' Penelope sighed.

As Diana and Bruce finished putting in the new watering system, Penelope and Conrad strolled up to them.

'Conrad has just got a new camera,' Penelope said to Bruce, hoping Baz had conveyed her message without any mix ups. 'He was wondering if he might take some shots of you.'

While Diana wasn't looking she strolled up to Bruce and whispered in his ear. 'Just make sure you show up in all his photos. And that's a wish.'

Bruce swatted.

'No worries. Go for your life, Conrad,' he said, crinkling his blue eyes as he smiled at the boy. 'I think this is my best profile.'

Conrad took some photos of Bruce. Then he took photographs of everyone else, as he didn't want to make it look too obvious that he was only interested in Bruce. Determined to see the developed photographs as soon as possible, he asked Penelope to get Mossop to drive them into town. The second the photos were ready he riffled through them.

'He's in every single photo,' he announced in amazement. 'He's even in the ones that he wasn't in.'

Mossop looked confused and Penelope looked concerned.

'Look at this,' Conrad whistled in astonishment. 'He's even in the shots I took at Christmas. I didn't even know him then.'

After that Conrad was more determined than ever to trap Bruce. Back at Townes Downs he coated the hall floor with flour while Penelope watched with a worried expression. Baz peered around the corner, spying on them with binoculars.

'If he's a ghost, he won't leave any footprints, right?' Conrad muttered to Penelope.

'He'll leave footprints,' Penelope replied grimly. 'I guarantee it.'

As Conrad continued to scatter flour, Penelope caught sight of Baz and grabbed him.

'Tell your dad to leave footprints,' she whispered. 'Understood?'

'Don't worry, Pen,' Baz assured her. 'You can count on me.'

Conrad hid himself and his camera inside a large overcoat hanging in the hall and settled down to wait. Before long Bruce appeared. Giving Penelope a cheeky grin he walked down the hall and left footprints all right – large tiger paw prints right down the length of the hall.

Conrad's eyes almost bugged out of his head. Then the front door was suddenly flung wide open, and a stampede of tourists rushed into the hall.

'The toilet's down there,' Otto yelled from the rear.

By the time the tourists had rushed through the hall the footprints were trampled and so too was Bruce. Knocked over in the rush, he sprawled on the floor. With white flour covering his face, hair and clothes, he struggled to his feet and lurched towards Conrad.

'Don't be scared,' he said with a chuckle to the bug-eyed boy. 'It's only flour. I'm not really a ghost.'

Conrad sprang into action and suddenly shoved a mirror up to Bruce's face in a desperate attempt to see if there was a reflection. Bruce however calmly used the mirror to fix his hair.

'Thank you,' he said cheerfully.

With a manic gleam in his eye, Conrad pulled a large magnet out of his pocket and held it to Bruce's head.

'I may have a magnetic personality, but really . . .' Bruce sighed.

'Okay,' Conrad hissed in frustration. 'You're not a robot-oid or a ghost but I know you're something. How come you don't ever eat, drink, bathe, blow your nose or attend to bodily functions?'

'He's very nervous about your personal hygiene, isn't he?' Mossop commented to Bruce. She and Diana had come into the hall where Conrad's performance had held them entranced. Conrad squirmed with embarrassment.

'You think you're so smart,' Conrad hissed at a grinning Bruce. 'But you haven't won yet, you phoney, pseudo-human non-human! I'm not giving up until I find out your secret.'

The next day at dawn, Conrad tied a bandanna Rambo-style around his head. Beside him in a tent at the camping ground, Baz stuck his finger in a tin of boot polish and tried to copy the camouflage design Conrad had painted on his face. Unfortunately he got carried away and painted his whole face black.

'What are we going to do now?' Baz asked.

'This is top secret,' Conrad told him. 'We're going to effect a Code X!'

'Wow!' cried Baz, although he had no idea what Code X meant. Conrad checked that he had his water bottle and compass. Then he and Baz climbed onto his motorcycle and he kick-started it. The engine revved into life and the bike roared off, speeding towards the horizon.

After a long ride Conrad and Baz came to a ravine. They stood at the edge of it, looking down the steep drop. Baz hopped up and down excitedly, thinking his adventure with Conrad was a great game. The older boy grinned at him, then reached for his mobile phone.

'I can't explain,' Conrad said when Mossop answered the phone. 'An apparition picked us up and took us out to the ravine.'

Conrad gestured to Baz, who happily started yelling.

'Help! Save me! I'm scared! The pigs are coming, the pigs are coming!'

Baz became so carried away that Conrad had to signal him to shut up.

'Wild pigs,' Conrad explained down the phone. 'Hungry savage boars.'

'And a big crocodile!' yelled Baz.

In the living room of the Townes Downs homestead, everyone was in a great panic as Mossop relayed the message from Conrad.

'They're at the edge of Townes Ravine!' she cried.

'Bruce, you mustn't panic,' Diana cried, throwing her arms around him. 'We'll save your little boy.'

Bruce tried not to smile. He liked being hugged by Diana, but the second she let go of him he quietly slipped away unnoticed.

'Tell Bruce only he can save us,' Conrad yelled down the phone. 'They're attacking. Aaaghhhh!'

Conrad simulated the sound of a great battle, then hung up and gave Baz a thin-lipped smile.

'We're at least thirty minutes by car from the house. If your dad shows up sooner, I'll have proof,' he announced.

'Hi, Dad,' Baz said casually. Conrad turned and screamed as a giant boulder turned into Bruce.

'G'day, son,' Bruce said. 'Where's the pig?'

Conrad stared at him stunned.

'Hey, Conrad,' Baz laughed. 'Watch this.'

Baz jumped over the edge of the ravine and Conrad screamed with horror, then screamed again in shock when

Baz cheerfully bounced back. Then, staring at Bruce and Baz in disbelief, he slowly blacked out.

Back at Townes Downs everyone piled into Otto's four-wheel-drive bus to go look for Baz and Conrad.

'There you are, Bruce,' Diana cried as he joined the search party, taking the seat next to her.

Diana held his hand comfortingly, although Penelope scowled at him, thinking he looked more contented than concerned. When they arrived at the ravine it was Bruce who suggested where they look. Penelope shot him a knowing look. She was sure he had already found the boys.

Sure enough, it wasn't long before the searchers stumbled across them, right where Bruce had suggested they'd be. Baz, tired out from his early morning adventure, was fast asleep. Beside him Conrad lay unconscious.

As Conrad slowly came round, his eyes had trouble focusing. Then he became aware that Bruce was watching him.

'He's a rock!' screamed Conrad. 'A big boulder!'

The others stared at him and then at each other in concern. Diana and Mossop assumed he must have slipped, hit his head on a rock and become concussed. Penelope glared at Bruce and Baz. She knew they must have played tricks on Conrad.

Otto watched his nephew with a frown. He was convinced Conrad had gone stark staring mad.

'Poor Conrad,' sighed Penelope. 'He can't tell the difference between a rock and a person.'

After his experience at the ravine, Conrad was quiet and subdued. Penelope thought he'd given up, but he hadn't. He'd just become sneakier. He spied on Bruce every chance he got, and was surprised one day to see Penelope, Bruce and Baz materialise out of thin air in the garden.

Keeping well hidden, he watched as Penelope threw a tantrum at Bruce. He'd been playing tricks again, twisting her wishes, and she was furious. Penelope took her opal pendant off and waved it angrily under Bruce's nose.

'See this,' she shouted. 'This means I'm your master. You're supposed to do what I say. And if you don't I'll just have to teach you a lesson.'

'Penelope,' called Diana crossly as she walked towards them from the house. 'I've told you before that you mustn't speak to people like that.'

Penelope almost screamed when she realised her mother had heard her. As she frantically tried to think up excuses, Conrad's phone rang. He dashed away before anyone heard it, and missed seeing Diana grab Penelope's opal out of her hands.

'You don't deserve nice things like this,' Diana said firmly. 'When you've learned how to talk properly to Bruce, you can have it back.'

Bruce and Baz looked at each other, both of them happy to have Diana as their master. Penelope glowered at Bruce.

'I'm sorry for being rude,' she said huffily then turned to her mother. 'Can I have my opal back now, please?'

'No,' Diana replied. 'That was a pathetic apology. Run along now, Penelope. Please help Mossie in the kitchen.'

Reluctantly Penelope backed off, giving Bruce a baleful

look. Bruce waved at her cockily and beside him little Baz jumped up and down with excitement. He adored Diana.

'A new master, dad!' he said happily. 'You've rubbed . . .'

Baz's voice became muffled as Bruce clapped a hand over his mouth.

'Not this time,' Bruce said softly, gazing at Diana and thinking how pretty she looked in the late afternoon light. 'Baz, why don't you go give Pen a hand?'

'But she's giving Mossie a hand,' Baz protested.

'Off you go, mate,' Bruce said giving him a nudge. 'There's a good bloke.'

Baz trudged after Penelope, feeling a little bit hurt that his father didn't want him around. Conrad, on the phone to his uncle, peeked out of his hiding place and saw the dejected little boy stomping his feet on his way up the front stairs of the house.

'I've apologised for Penelope so many times,' Diana murmured to Bruce.

'Oh, it's nothing,' Bruce muttered. 'Um, beautiful sunset.'

Diana looked towards the west. Night was beginning to fall but the sky was simply grey, with no sunset colours.

'It's not really,' Diana said smiling at Bruce. 'I wish it really was beautiful.'

Bruce swatted casually, as if he was brushing off a mosquito, and the sky became pink and golden then red. Diana was surprised and delighted and she and Bruce stayed in the garden, watching the changing colours.

In the house, Baz was depressed. He scuffed his feet, lonely without his father, and was surprised when Penelope made one of her rare attempts to be nice to him.

'Baz,' she said. 'We have to do something about your father and my mother. Isn't there some magic you could use to get him away from her?'

'How far away?' Baz asked.

'Not far. The moon, maybe. Come on, Baz,' Penelope said wheedlingly. 'You're my favourite little genie. Couldn't you give me one wish?'

Behind the door, Conrad almost rustled with excitement. His spying was paying off. So Bruce and Baz were genies!

'You're not our master any more,' Baz told Penelope.

'Perhaps you could give me a freebie,' Penelope said, giving Baz a smile that was supposed to be warm but looked sickly.

'It's against the rules,' Baz told her honestly.

Penelope gritted her teeth.

'Come on,' she urged. 'For old times' sake. I mean, he got rid of you, didn't he. Pushed you aside to be with my mother.'

Baz thought about it and miserably realised it was true.

'Yeah,' he said. 'But I still can't give you a wish.'

Down at the camping grounds, a group of elderly men complained about the quality of food they were getting on their Von Meister Tour.

'Shut up and get back to your tent,' Otto bellowed. When he wasn't sucking up to the Towneses to get near the opal, he wasn't at all nice. Conrad rushed towards him, out of breath with excitement.

'Uncle, it's about the opal,' he panted.

Otto's eyes gleamed and he put his arm around Conrad. 'What about it?' he asked eagerly.

'It's magic,' Conrad explained. 'Bruce and Baz are genies.'

The light died in Otto's eyes and he took his arm off Conrad's shoulders. He was now absolutely positive that Conrad was demented.

'Did something hit you on the head again?' he asked.

'No,' Conrad quivered at his uncle's tone. 'I saw them appear out of nowhere!'

Giving Conrad a glance that chilled his blood, Otto stormed off to make life even more hellish for the tourists. Conrad realised he was going to need more proof before he could convince his uncle. He slunk back towards the house.

In the morning, cramped from hiding in a bush, Conrad saw Bruce walk towards the house, tailed enthusiastically by Baz.

'Where are we going, Dad?' Baz asked eagerly.

'Look, mate,' Bruce replied carelessly. 'Do you reckon you could just amuse yourself this morning?'

'Don't you want me around any more?' Baz asked pathetically. Bruce looked at him guiltily, but he had other things on his mind.

'Of course I do,' he said kindly. 'I'll see you later, okay?'

Sadly Baz watched his dad walk away. Then, choosing his moment carefully, Conrad leapt out from behind a bush.

'G'day, mate. How are you?' Conrad asked in a friendly voice.

Baz looked around in confusion to see who Conrad was talking to, but no-one else was around.

'How's it going, little buddy?' Conrad asked with a smile that reminded Baz of a shark.

'What do you want?' Baz asked. Conrad was never friendly to him. Never, ever, ever.

'I just thought my good mate might be interested in a bit of fun for a change,' Conrad said, squinting thoughtfully at the small boy.

'Who's your good mate?' Baz asked.

'You are, mate,' Conrad told him. 'You're my good mate!'

Diana changed her clothes to go riding with Bruce while Penelope begged her to return the opal.

'Please, can I have my opal back now?' she implored. 'I'm being polite. I used the word please.'

Diana put her hand into a pocket and pulled the opal pendant out. Penelope reached towards it.

'I'm holding onto it,' Diana told her.

'Why?' Penelope howled.

'I don't think you've really learned your lesson yet,' Diana replied. 'Bye, darling.'

'Where are you going?' Penelope asked her mother as she followed her outside.

'Riding with Bruce,' Diana replied.

'Wait!' cried Penelope.

'I do wish you'd be quiet,' her mother said.

Bruce waved in Penelope's direction and she fell silent although her mouth still flapped. Full of silent protests she followed Bruce and Diana to a shed where Diana pointed to two trail bikes.

'I found these earlier and thought they would be most amusing,' she said.

Bruce nodded and Penelope glared as they climbed on the bikes and took off, laughing happily. They'd only gone a short distance when they came across Otto's bus bogged in a creek bed. While Otto revved the engine, exhausted elderly tourists pushed and heaved at the bus trying to get it free.

'We shouldn't be doing this. We paid for a holiday,' shouted one of the tired tourists.

'I should be charging you extra for this experience,' Otto retorted. Then he saw Bruce and Diana come to a stop nearby.

'G'day, Di,' he called, turning on his greasy charm. 'How's that charming daughter of yours? And her beautiful opal?'

'Mister Meister,' Diana replied coldly. 'Quite frankly it's not your concern how my daughter is. I do wish you'd mind your own business.'

Bruce casually waved as they rode off and Otto suddenly jumped out of the bus and rushed to stop the tourists.

'Don't do that,' he roared. 'Let me do it. It's *my* business.'

Disconsolately Penelope wandered around Townes Downs, trying to find Baz to see if she could shake just one little act of magic out of him. But she couldn't find him anywhere.

Penelope didn't know that Conrad had taken Baz into town, where he was treating the little genie to every ride at the fun park. First they went on the merry-go-round, then Conrad bought Baz a balloon. Next they wandered through the Hall of Horrors, then rode the Big Dipper. Finally, by the time they came to the dodgem cars, Baz truly believed that Conrad was his mate.

'Let me get this straight,' Conrad said conversationally, as if it was no big deal. 'If I had the opal you'd have to do everything I say, right?'

'Yeah,' replied Baz, looking around at the attractions. Conrad followed him over to a series of distorting mirrors that made them look tall and skinny or short and fat.

'Conrad, I'm having the best time,' Baz said happily.

'What are mates for!' Conrad replied.

Baz looked up at the older boy. His dad had ignored him but Conrad had made sure he was happy. 'I'd like to repay you,' he said.

'Gee,' Conrad drawled. 'I can't think of anything I need . . . Unless maybe . . .'

'What, mate? Just name it,' Baz cried.

'Well, I haven't got a magic opal,' Conrad said sadly.

Baz squirmed uncomfortably.

'Can you get it off Penelope for your best mate?' Conrad coaxed.

'Penelope hasn't got the opal,' Baz replied. Conrad was thunderstruck, but he tried not to show it.

'Who has?'

'I can't tell you who my master is now,' Baz replied. 'It's

one of the rules of magic.'

Conrad pretended to understand but he didn't give up.

'Not even for a mate?' he urged. 'Couldn't you give a mate the opal?'

Baz shook his head. 'I can't even pick the opal up, let alone give it to you. Anyway, Dad'd kill me.'

Conrad wasn't going to let all his hard work and hard earned savings go to waste.

'Your dad,' he said softly. 'You mean the guy who didn't want you around.'

Baz looked sad and Conrad put his arm around him.

'Baz, don't you see? I'd be a great master. You want to stay in Australia? That'd be my first wish. Anything you want, I'd wish for. We're a team!'

Baz nodded at Conrad and smiled. He wanted to help him but he wasn't sure how.

Bruce and Diana rode the trail bikes out to a large lake where they strolled on the shore admiring the view. Lady Diana Townes couldn't remember ever having so much fun with her stuffy friends back in England. She smiled warmly at the tall, fair man beside her.

'Isn't this wonderful,' sighed Diana. 'It's so nice to be here with you.'

'Yes, it is,' he replied. 'Without Penelope.'

'I wish she could see this,' Diana commented.

Bruce waved and Penelope suddenly appeared behind them. Her mouth worked furiously although she made no sound.

'Fancy seeing you out here, darling,' Diana greeted her. 'I do wish you'd speak up.'

Bruce waved and Penelope's volume was suddenly turned up full.

'You dare to use magic to cast a spell over my mother,' she yelled. 'I know you want to be free, but how could you stoop so low?'

Diana was furious with her and turned to Bruce.

'I constantly wish she was more polite,' she exclaimed.

Bruce swatted and Penelope's manner instantly changed.

'Oh, I am sorry,' Penelope cooed. 'Please forgive me. Was I interrupting something?'

That night, back at Townes Downs, Diana changed her clothes for dinner. She left her jacket, with the opal pendant in the pocket, on the coat stand in the hall. She, Bruce and Penelope dined together in the candlelit dining room. It would have been very romantic if it wasn't for Penelope. Spotting Bruce throwing his food out the window when Diana wasn't looking, she decided to be difficult.

'Don't you like the food, Bruce?' she asked.

'Sorry,' Bruce replied. 'I was just giving a snack to a passing possum.'

'But you've hardly touched your meal,' Diana commented. Penelope smiled when she saw Bruce squirm.

'I'm trying to lose a few pounds,' he explained.

'Bruce, you look fine to me,' Diana said, gazing at him in a way that made Penelope want to puke. 'Doesn't he look fine to you, Penelope?'

'Magic,' she replied sourly.

Diana looked thoughtfully at her daughter.

'I do wish you'd say what's bothering you.'

Bruce was about to wave when he realised that Diana didn't have the opal.

'Since you asked, mother,' Penelope replied coldly. 'I don't like you sitting so close to Bruce.'

'He's on the other side of the table. What do you mean?' Diana asked.

'I don't like the idea of you getting romantically involved with another man,' Penelope declared as she and Diana stared at each other.

'Well, that's cleared up,' Bruce announced in an embarrassed voice. Then he changed the subject. 'I wonder what Mossop has for dessert?'

Penelope ignored him and continued addressing her mother.

'When you were going to marry Bubbles, it was all right. It was a financial arrangement. But this is different.'

Bruce squirmed uncomfortably and Diana was surprised and sad. Penelope obviously meant what she said. Diana didn't want to upset her, but she didn't want to lose Bruce either.

'Has anyone seen Baz today?' Bruce asked loudly, but neither Diana nor Penelope appeared to be listening.

'I feel like I'm losing my mummy . . .' Penelope said sadly.

Conrad and Baz peered into the dining room when they arrived home. Baz felt hurt and a little jealous that his Dad was with Diana and Penelope. Conrad noticed the look on his face and smiled craftily. Then he pretended to look concerned.

'I suppose your dad forgot to invite you,' he whispered so no-one in the dining room could hear him. 'Don't worry about it, mate. You've still got me.'

'Yeah,' Baz said. He felt like crying.

'So, mate, where's the opal?' Conrad whispered.

Baz knew he wasn't supposed to tell, but Conrad had been such a good friend he decided it would be all right to drop a hint.

'There might be something around here that interests you,' he mumbled.

Conrad got the hint and started looking around. He spotted the coat stand and crept over to it.

'Here?' he asked.

'I can't say,' Baz told him.

Conrad started going through the coats.

'Come on, Baz. Give me a hint.'

'You're getting warm,' Baz replied.

Conrad pounced on Diana's jacket, thrust his hand in the pocket and pulled out the opal. With a power-crazed expression he started rubbing it.

'You've got the opal in your hand,' Baz announced. 'Your every wish is our command.'

'About time too,' Conrad muttered.

Diana had left the table to help Mossop in the kitchen with the desserts. Penelope looked miserably at Bruce.

'I know I don't have the opal,' she said. 'But I wish you weren't here.'

Bruce suddenly vanished and Penelope's jaw dropped with amazement. Diana came back into the dining room and looked around in surprise.

'Where did Bruce go?' she asked.

'I'll try to find him,' Penelope cried, rushing from the table.

She found Bruce, Baz and Conrad under the house.

'What's going on, son?' Bruce was asking Baz. He was unhappy to see that Conrad had the opal. Penelope was horrified.

'What's he doing with the opal?' she stammered.

'Just making a few wishes,' Conrad told her with a gleam in his eye. 'Bye bye, Pen.'

'What do you mean?' she cried.

'I wish you Poms were all back in England right now!' he replied with a manic laugh.

Bruce swatted and Penelope and Diana found themselves sitting at the grand dining table at Townes Hall. Mossop came into the elegant dining room.

'Would you like cream on your dessert?' she asked as the three looked at each other in confusion.

'Okay, genies. Work time!' Conrad snapped. Bruce and Baz looked at each other unhappily. The first wish was for a gymnasium. As Conrad checked out the brand new equipment that materialised, Bruce took Baz aside for a chat.

'You've really done it this time, son,' Bruce muttered. 'I've told you a hundred times . . .'

'When?' Baz cried. 'Not lately. You told me to go and amuse myself.'

'What's that got to do with it?' Bruce asked. 'It's not important right now.'

'It's important to me!' Baz wailed.

Bruce looked at him guiltily.

'Sorry, Baz. You're right.'

'It's okay, Dad,' Baz assured him. 'Conrad said he'd do what we want. Me and him are mates.'

'Mates? With him?' Bruce cried, not believing what he was hearing.

Baz turned to Conrad.

'Dad doesn't believe you'll do anything for us,' he said. 'So why don't you take us to the cave where the opal was found? Just to show Dad we're mates.'

'Mate,' sneered Conrad. 'We *could* go up to that cave and get inside the opal and you and your dad would finally be free. But that would be too easy.'

Bruce realised Baz had let slip all their secrets. Baz's face fell as he realised that maybe he shouldn't have trusted Conrad.

'But you said . . .' Baz began but Conrad only smirked at his distress.

'Dad, he said he'd do it. He did,' Baz wailed.

'It's okay, Baz,' Bruce said soothingly as he comforted the small genie.

'Baz, go play by yourself,' Conrad ordered. 'Your father and I have work to do.'

In cold rainy England, Diana looked at Penelope with a tear in her eye.

'I'm sorry, Penelope,' she said. 'I didn't mean to make you feel left out.'

'Oh, Mummy, what a mess, and it's all my fault,' Penelope replied miserably. She hated seeing her mother so sad. Why shouldn't Diana have some love in her life? She made a promise to herself that if she ever got hold of the opal again she'd let Bruce and Diana fall in love without interfering.

'I'm really sorry, Dad,' Baz said mournfully. Before Bruce could comfort him, Conrad demanded another wish.

'I wish I had a circus right here, right now,' he demanded.

Bruce tiredly waved and a small box appeared.

'It's a flea circus,' he explained.

'Very funny,' snapped Conrad. 'I wish for a real circus. Clowns, lions . . .'

Bruce looked exhausted, but he waved and clowns tumbled across the floor and from somewhere very nearby lions roared loudly.

'Conrad, there are limits to my powers,' Bruce sighed.

'Then I'll just wish there are no limits. Simple eh? Conrad scoffed.

'It's like a battery running down. I can't last forever,' Bruce said, sounding drained. Baz looked at him in worry, but Conrad just didn't care.

'I wish for a tribe of Neanderthal men,' he ordered. 'And a dinosaur.'

Bruce, utterly exhausted, began to grow transparent. Baz timidly approached Conrad the tyrant.

'Conrad, wouldn't it be good if that bossy boots Penelope could see you now?' he suggested.

'Brilliant, Baz! What a good idea. She'd be green with envy. I wish Penelope would drop in!'

Bruce waved weakly and Penelope landed right on top of Conrad. They crashed to the floor in a heap. The pendant flew from Conrad's hand and they both grabbed it.

'I wish she'd let go,' Conrad grunted as they tussled.

'I wish he'd let go,' Penelope shrieked.

'Two masters,' Bruce commented. 'That's never happened before.'

Otto suddenly barged into the room, sending Penelope, Conrad and the opal flying.

'What's going on, Conrad?' he roared.

Conrad looked up at him, and at the same moment Penelope lost her balance and slipped. They both dropped the pendant. When they looked around, the opal had vanished.

'Where's the opal?' Conrad cried frantically.

'They can't have it,' Penelope said, pointing at Bruce and Baz. 'They can't even touch it.'

Then she realised Bruce didn't look too comfortable sitting on the floor. Realising he must be sitting on it, she tugged at his arm. Conrad immediately grabbed his other arm.

'I thought you were exhausted,' Baz said to his dad.

'Can't you tell when I'm acting? Help me, Baz!' Bruce cried.

As Conrad, Penelope and Otto shoved Bruce aside and dived for the opal, Baz held up the box containing the flea circus. Otto had no idea what was happening, but he realised Penelope and Conrad were eyeing the box with dread.

'Don't move,' yelled Baz.

'Come on, mate,' Conrad wheedled. 'You've got to do the right thing by your mates.'

'You're right,' Baz declared. He opened the flea circus and dumped the contents onto Conrad and Otto. They immediately began to itch and scratch.

Penelope grabbed the opal.

'Thanks, Baz,' she said.

'No worries, Pen,' Baz replied.

Penelope waved the opal in front of Otto and Conrad.

'You're both getting very forgetful,' she murmured.

'What do you mean?' Otto grunted. 'I have a memory like an elephant.'

'Really!' cried Penelope. 'Well, I have a magic genie, and I wish everyone would forget about this incident!'

Bruce swatted and Conrad and Otto suddenly couldn't remember what they were doing there or why they were itching. Mossop and Diana reappeared, having no idea that they had been away. But Diana seemed to be sad, as if she'd lost something special.

That evening, Bruce shyly approached her as she stood on the verandah watching the sunset.

'G'day, Di,' he said. 'I love a good sunset.'

'So do I,' sighed Diana. 'They remind me of something but I can't remember what.'

Bruce's shoulders drooped. Diana had forgotten their romance. From the doorway, Penelope watched them. She nabbed little Baz as he headed out to join them.

'I wish you'd let Bruce and my mother be alone,' she whispered, hoping that maybe by themselves they'd find romance again and her mother would be happy.

Baz nodded. Alone! That was easy, he could do that. Casually he swatted. Diana found herself *alone* on one side of the veranda, while Bruce stood *alone* on the opposite side of the house.

Chapter Ten

'By rights that opal is ours, Conrad,' Otto muttered. 'And if we had it, it'd bring us nothing but good luck.'

Conrad squinted thoughtfully at the photograph Otto was holding. It was a picture of a smug-looking Penelope wearing her opal pendant. Conrad gazed around at the filthy bus and then at the small dusty town where Von Meister Tours was based. The Von Meisters could certainly do with some good luck.

'I don't suppose this is where we sign on for the tour?' cried a voice with an English accent.

Conrad glanced up. A group of English tourists, including a pair of twins, clustered hopefully around Otto.

'This is a very busy time of year,' Otto told them. 'I'll check with my booking clerk.'

Otto thrust his head inside the bus and found Trish asleep on one of the seats.

'Trish,' he bellowed. 'Are there any cancellations for the next outback experience?'

'There aren't any bookings,' Trish replied. 'So how can there be any cancellations?'

Otto glared at her then turned to the tourists with a smarmy smile.

'You're very lucky people. Trish will sign you up for an outback experience you'll never forget.'

Conrad looked at the middle-aged twins and thought they were total Pommy prats. They had dorky accents and fish-belly white legs, but something about them began to trigger an idea.

'Uncle Otto,' he whispered excitedly. 'I know how we can get that opal off Penelope. We'll get another opal – an identical one – and we'll swap it with hers.'

Otto's eyes gleamed for just a moment. Then he looked scornfully at his nephew.

'It's a stupid idea, Conrad. It'll never work.'

'But Otto . . .' Conrad began. He was interrupted by another Pommy prat.

'Hello,' called Bubbles, bustling towards them in a safari suit. 'I'm Lord Akryngton-Smythe. I'm trying to get to Townes Downs.'

'You've come to the right place,' Otto said. 'I've got one first-class seat left on the bus.'

'Oh, capital,' cried Bubbles. He eyed the filthy old bus dubiously. 'What's the difference between first and second class?'

'You get a cushion in first class,' Otto replied.

All the way to Townes Downs, the passengers complained about the uncomfortable seats, the lack of air conditioning and the unbearable body odour of the driver. When the bus finally arrived, Bubbles was the first to stagger off it, dirty, dishevelled and distressed.

'Lucky I went first class,' he mumbled, sure he wouldn't have survived anything less.

'No worries, Acky,' Otto said casually.

Diana and Penelope were amazed to see Bubbles, who swayed on his feet then, utterly exhausted, fell flat on his face in the dirt. Diana and Penelope helped him up to the house and Diana spoon fed him soup to help him regain some strength.

'I couldn't stop thinking about you, Diana,' Bubbles explained. 'You know how I feel. I've come all the way from England to tell you that I'm prepared to meet you half way.'

'Half way would be India,' Diana said, popping another spoonful of soup into his mouth before he could say anything more.

That night Mossop tucked Penelope into bed.

'Don't forget it's Mothers' Day the day after tomorrow,' she said. 'I hope you've got your mother a nice present.'

'Don't worry. It's all taken care of,' Penelope assured her. With a magic opal *everything* was taken of. Bruce kept telling her she was getting lazy, but Penelope didn't care. As soon as Mossop had left the room she rubbed the opal and Bruce and Baz instantly appeared.

'What did you get your mum?' Baz asked interestedly. He adored Diana and if she was his own mother he would plan a special gift.

'I'll think of something and you can get it for me,' Penelope replied carelessly, then began giving orders.

'I wish to fall into a deep sleep immediately and wake up at exactly eight-forty-five am. Not a second before or after. And I wish to dream about being on a desert island.'

Bruce waved and Penelope immediately fell into a deep sleep. She didn't stir some time later when Conrad crept into her room. He leaned over her bed and gently lifted her up and eased the opal pendant over her head, replacing it with a fake pendant from a tourist shop in town.

Penelope thudded back on to the pillow and Conrad

quietly tiptoed from the room. In the hallway he rubbed the opal admiringly.

'You've rubbed the opal . . .' Baz said cheerfully.

Conrad gawped at him. He had no memory of the opal being the home of the genies and thought it was very unlucky that Baz and Bruce had found him outside Penelope's room with her opal in his hand.

'I s'pose you're wondering why I was in Penelope's room just then . . .' he mumbled as he tried to think of a way to explain and escape with the opal.

Before he had a chance to say anything more, Mossop came around the corner in the hall and bumped into him. She'd heard noises and had gone to investigate. Seeing Penelope's opal in Conrad's hands she grabbed it quickly.

'Playing practical jokes at this time of night!' she exclaimed crossly. 'Off you go. Out!'

'I was just having a chat to Bruce and Baz,' Conrad said, acting weaselly under Mossop's glare. Mossop looked around. Bruce and Baz were nowhere in sight.

'Good night,' she said firmly, marching him to the front door and showing him out. Sleepily she rubbed the opal and was surprised to find Bruce and Baz standing right behind her.

'You've rubbed the opal in your hand . . .' Baz began.

'Where did you two come from?' she asked. 'Sssh. Lord Akryngton-Smythe is resting in there.'

She pointed to the room where Bubbles slept.

'I wish he was up and about again,' she commented.

Bubbles, woken from a bad dream, suddenly stuck his head around the door of the spare bedroom.

131

'Please don't put me back on the bus,' he whimpered. 'I'm allergic to Ottos. No more bus.'

'It's all right, your lordship,' Mossop soothed.

Otto, being overweight, had difficulty climbing through Penelope's bedroom window, but eventually he made it.

'Coconuts,' Penelope murmured.

Otto, fearing that he'd woken her, immediately put his hands out in front of him and pretended to be sleepwalking. Then he looked more closely and realised Penelope was sound asleep.

He shook her slightly but she continued to sleep and he smiled as he swapped the opal around her neck for the one he pulled from his pocket.

Back at the camping ground, he thrust a pendant under a sulking Conrad's nose.

'Conrad, I'm a genius,' Otto said modestly. 'Look what I've got.'

'How did you get that?' Conrad asked. 'I had it but she took it off me.'

'And I took it off her,' Otto said smugly. 'What Otto wants, Otto gets. This opal is going to change our luck, you mark my words.'

Excited and happy, they hugged each other and the tent collapsed around them.

At a quarter past nine the next morning, Penelope woke up and looked at her alarm clock.

'I slept in late! I don't believe it,' she said crossly and rubbed her opal to summon Bruce and Baz.

Nothing happened and she rubbed it more vigorously.

'This is an official wish, Bruce,' she muttered angrily. 'I want you here right now. And I'm only going to give you one more chance!'

Still nothing happened.

'Right, that's it,' she fumed. 'I'll just have to . . .'

Then the awful truth dawned on her. If Bruce and Baz didn't answer her summons, she'd just have to do a lot of things for herself. Without the genies as her servants, she'd have to find her own clean clothes to wear. She'd have to do her own hair. She'd even have to clean her own teeth.

A little later she came out on to the verandah and found Bruce lazing in a hammock. She spluttered with fury.

'Why aren't you obeying me?' she demanded. 'Why haven't you been granting my wishes.'

'I didn't hear you make any wishes,' Bruce grinned and stretched lazily. 'Maybe your opal doesn't work any more.'

'Are you saying the magic has run out?' Penelope cried disbelievingly. She rubbed the opal frantically.

'I wish you'd bring me my tea and toast,' she commanded.

'Sorry Pen,' Bruce yawned. 'You'll just have to help yourself.'

'This is one of your tricks, isn't it?' she huffed.

Baz wandered out on to the verandah. He'd been having a lot of fun granting Mossop's wishes. Mossop had wished

133

for a beautiful chocolate cake for Diana for Mothers' Day, and Baz had thoroughly enjoyed helping in the kitchen.

'Son, how much magic is in that opal?' Bruce asked and gestured to the fake opal around Penelope's neck.

'Absolutely none,' Baz replied. Although Penelope didn't trust Bruce, she could tell Baz was being honest.

'You mean the magic's really gone?' Penelope wailed, so sadly she was almost sobbing. 'I'll have to do everything myself!'

In despair she went to the kitchen where she burnt several slices of toast trying to make her own breakfast.

Baz and Bruce watched the wisps of smoke curl their way out through the kitchen window.

'She doesn't know Mossop has the real opal,' Bruce explained to Baz. 'And we're not allowed to tell her. That's the rules.'

Mossop dourly examined the growing pile of burnt toast.

'Are you still going to make breakfast for your mother tomorrow morning?' she asked doubtfully. On the previous day, when she still had her magic opal, Penelope had boasted that she was going to make her mother the best breakfast ever.

'Yes, it's going to be very special,' Penelope muttered. Then she gave up on the toast and decided to have a banana for breakfast instead.

At the camping ground, Otto was convinced he had the lucky opal. Two flat tyres on the bus hadn't changed his mind.

'No need to worry,' he said to Conrad. 'Any minute now our luck will start to change. I can feel it.'

Conrad wasn't so sure. He could feel rumblings of discontent coming from the tourists and he wasn't surprised when a deputation of angry Englishmen arrived, led by Bubbles.

'We'd just like you to know,' Bubbles said firmly, 'that we're unhappy with the catering, the accommodation, the transport, the lack of air conditioning in the bus, and the lack of suspension under the bus.'

The other tourists cheered him on. Bubbles continued as Otto glared at him angrily.

'Your personal habits are disgusting. Your body odour makes us all feel sick. Your language, and your attitude, leave a lot to be desired.'

'Yeah, but apart from what you just said, does anyone have any genuine complaints?' Otto said malevolently.

'Your food is hardly fit for human consumption,' one of the twins said timidly. The fat Australian tour operator smelt like a wild animal and that scared him.

'I mean, it's just like what we get at home in England,' the twin added, becoming increasingly nervous as Otto glared at him.

'I'm jack of you lot,' Otto bellowed. 'I'm going to hand you over to Trish. She's in charge of the whingeing Pom department.'

Otto clambered into the bus and Bubbles and the tourists banged on the door.

'I'm Otto's representative,' Trish said loyally. 'Whatever you want to say to him, you can say to me.'

'We want to kill him,' one of the twins cried.

'He's in there!' Trish said quickly as she leapt out of the way. But by the time the tourists charged into the bus, they found Otto had climbed out the other side and disappeared.

'A chap can run but he cannot hide from justice,' Bubbles exclaimed. 'We'll find him.'

Led by Bubbles, the tourists rushed into the bush to hunt Otto down.

'Bruce, I've been thinking about the opal, and how much I've come to rely on it,' Penelope said slowly. 'Please hold out your hand.'

Bruce held out his hand. Penelope dropped the opal into it. Instead of it passing right through Bruce's palm, he held it with no problems.

'That was the final test,' Penelope said softly. 'If you can hold it, then the magic is really gone.'

'Magic is a difficult thing to handle,' Bruce said, squirming at Penelope's dismay.

Penelope stared at the opal and made an important decision. Suddenly she threw it as far away as she could.

'There!' she cried. 'I don't have to think about it any more. 'It's all in the past now.'

At sunset, Bubbles and the other tourists were still straggling through the bush in search of Otto. Despite their exhaustion, they all felt proud of their endeavours. This was a true outback experience.

Penelope watched the darkening skies from the verandah. Her life had been touched by magic, but now she'd
lost it. The thought of doing things for herself made her
feel older, wiser and more mature – but sadder, too.

In the morning, Mossop offered to make up a breakfast
tray for Penelope to take to her mother.

'No, thanks, Mossie,' Penelope replied. 'It's Mothers'
Day. It's not right if I don't make the breakfast.'

Mossop looked at her in surprise. This didn't sound like
the spoilt Penelope talking.

'Mossie, I've been trying to make Mummy a present, but
I can't seem to do anything right without . . .'

Penelope's voice trailed off. Baz burst into the kitchen,
erupting with excitement. Behind him Bruce entered
carrying a large card made from a piece of bark, and deco-
rated with leaves, flowers, twigs, feathers and stones.

'We've got the card for you,' Baz babbled. 'It's great. Your
mum's going to love it.'

'What do you reckon? Fantastic or what?' Bruce asked.

Penelope examined it carefully. To her it looked terribly
Australian with its strange bits of flora.

'We've been up all night finishing it,' Baz explained.

'It's very bizarre . . .' Penelope said.

'Dad, does that mean she likes it?' Baz asked.

'I don't think so,' Bruce replied.

'Thank you ever so much,' Penelope said. Then she
added sincerely. 'But even if I did like it, I wouldn't be able
to give it to Mummy. It has to be something I made
myself.'

137

Bruce and Baz looked at her and at each other in amazement. This didn't sound like Penelope.

'And it should be something she'd like,' she added.

'So what are you going to give her?' Baz asked.

Penelope grimaced. 'I don't know.'

While searching Townes Downs for his uncle, Conrad stumbled on the pendant that Penelope had thrown away. He shoved it in his pocket. Then he realised that he could smell something strong and familiar, an odour wafting from the shed. Quickly he sneaked inside.

'Otto? Uncle Otto?' he called in a whisper.

'Sssh, they'll hear you,' Otto whispered back. 'Those whingeing mongrels. Give them everything and it's still not enough.'

'Look what I found,' Conrad said, dangling the pendant in front of Otto's nose.

Otto was stunned when he saw the opal. He whipped out a jeweller's glass and examined it closely.

'This is a phoney,' he grunted.

'Oh!' exclaimed Conrad. 'It must have been the one I left with Penelope.'

'What do you mean?' Otto demanded.

'I didn't know that Mossop was going to spring me and get the real opal,' Conrad explained. 'But it's all right because you got the real opal off Mossop.'

'What do you mean Mossop?' Otto asked. 'I got this opal off Penelope.'

Conrad examined Otto's opal.

'It's a phoney too,' he said sourly.

'When you took the opal off Penelope, did you replace it with a phoney one?' Conrad asked.

'Of course I did,' Otto relied. 'What do you think I am. Stupid?'

'I thought you said it was a bad idea to swap opals,' Conrad accused.

'I meant it was a bad idea for you,' Otto declared. 'But it was a good idea for me because I'm more mature and trustworthy.'

Conrad had another idea.

'Otto, why don't we take these two opals to Mossop and ask if she wants to swap? Two for one. What do you think?'

'It's another stupid idea,' Otto growled. 'It'll never work.'

Penelope entered her mother's bedroom carrying a sprig of wattle from the garden.

'Happy Mothers' Day,' she said miserably. 'I'm sorry I don't have a present for you.'

She gazed at Diana sadly.

'I should have had one for you. You're the best mother in the world, but I'm just too spoilt and selfish to even organise one. I'm sorry, but I do love you, Mummy.'

Penelope hugged Diana and gave her a kiss. Diana looked at her, delighted.

'Penelope, this is the best Mothers' Day present you've ever given me.'

'Really!' cried Penelope cheering up. 'I could have done this ages ago.'

In the kitchen, Mossop pottered around preparing breakfast. She looked up with a frown when Otto and Conrad knocked at the door and came in.

'Missie Mossie, how are you?' Otto asked smoothly. 'Might I say how particularly well you're looking this morning.'

'What do you want?' she asked suspiciously. Sensing that something was up, Bruce and Baz ambled into the kitchen.

'You know that opal that I found in the corridor, that you took from me . . .' Conrad mumbled.

'Oooh,' cried Mossie. 'I was going to give that back to Miss Penelope. I forgot.'

'So you've still got it?' Otto enquired.

'Oh yes,' Mossie replied, patting her pocket. 'It's right here.'

'Isn't that amazing!' Otto said.

'Incredible,' added Conrad.

'What is?' Mossop asked.

'It's just that I found this opal out in the paddock,' said Conrad, dangling the fake pendant in front of him. Otto pretended to be surprised.

'Well, I'll be buttered on both sides. Look what I found out in the shed.'

Otto showed Mossop his fake opal. In confusion she took Penelope's opal out of her pocket.

'There's three of them,' she said in wonder.

Otto rubbed his hands together in glee. He thought it was going to be easy to get Mossop to swap the real opal for the two fakes. But just at that moment Penelope entered the room.

'What's going on?' she asked.

Before Mossop had a chance to reply, Otto sneezed. It was a huge, body-heaving sneeze and, accidently on purpose, he bumped into Conrad and Mossop and sent the opals flying.

Penelope, Mossop, Otto and Conrad immediately dived for the opals, trying to push each other out of the way in a flurry of arms and legs.

'Excuse me, Mister Meister,' Mossop yelled. 'Do you mind?'

'Give me that opal, it's mine,' bellowed Otto.

'How dare you touch me!' screamed Penelope.

Diana came running when she heard the yells.

'Stop this at once!' she shouted.

Penelope held tight on to one opal and, hoping it was the right one, rubbed it vigorously as she glared at Otto and Conrad.

'I wish you two would just get out of here,' she muttered.

Penelope looked hopefully at Bruce but he shook his head.

'Yeah, well, I just wish you'd drop on your head,' Otto growled at her. He waved the opal he was holding.

Penelope winced and covered her head, but nothing happened. She stared at Conrad, who held the third opal. She was about to jump on him and wrestle it from him when Bubbles and the English tourists burst into the room.

'On behalf of the oppressed tourists of the world . . .' Bubbles began.

141

'I wish you tourists would all just nick off back to Pommyland,' Conrad said hotly.

Penelope watched as Bruce swatted.

'We've all come to say goodbye,' Bubbles said politely. 'We're going back to England. Goodbye Diana.'

Diana stared astonished as Bubbles led the tourists out. She'd thought she was going to have a problem getting rid of him, but he seemed happy to go.

'We'll be off too,' Otto muttered and he and Conrad ran out the back door.

Penelope watched Conrad go with a sigh. He had the opal, but at least he didn't know it was magic. Baz smiled happily at the bark picture he and his father had made for Diana. Mossop had hung it up on a wall and Diana walked over and admired it.

'Penelope, wherever did you find this picture?' she asked.

'It's nothing, Mummy,' Penelope replied. 'I knew you wouldn't like it.'

'It's superb,' said Diana. 'It's a great work of art.'

Bruce smiled modestly. 'It's just something that Baz and I knocked up while we were boiling the billy.'

Diana smiled warmly at Bruce and Baz. Penelope fumed. Diana was making a fuss of the two genies, and they hadn't even used magic to make her happy.

I'll never take the opal for granted again, Penelope thought to herself. *Especially now that I don't have it.*

Chapter Eleven

Penelope paced along the wooden verandah at Townes Downs thinking hard. Somehow she had to get the opal back from Conrad before he realised it was magic. She was deep in thought when a voice interrupted her.

'You know what I think?' Conrad said, cracking a smile at her dismay. 'I think this opal is magic.'

Penelope gasped. She'd been transported into the dusty back room of the Von Meister tourist office, where Bruce and Baz hung around their new master. Despite all the evidence, Penelope decided to deny everything. She hoped that maybe she could somehow grab the opal and put everything back to normal again.

'Magic! Don't be stupid,' she snapped.

'I reckon Bruce are Baz are genies,' Conrad said teasingly.

'Genies! That's ridiculous,' Penelope retorted.

'I wish I had a new pair of Duke Floats,' Conrad said as he smirked at her.

Bruce swatted and a brand new, very flash-looking pair of shoes appeared on Conrad's feet.

'Here ya go, Penelope,' swaggered Conrad. 'Do you want a go?'

He held the opal out in front of Penelope. When she tried to snatch it, he pulled the opal away and laughed in her face.

'You're the most selfish, inconsiderate person I have ever met,' Penelope stormed. Conrad just laughed again.

'You're pretty selfish yourself,' he replied.

Bruce leaned down towards Baz.

'We have to get him up to that cave and into the opal,' he whispered.

'Right,' Baz nodded.

'First we'll lull him into a false sense of security,' Bruce whispered. 'We'll grant his wishes until he trusts us.'

In the front room of the tourist office a large woman made enquiries about the outback experience tours.

'What's the deluxe package?' she asked.

'Well,' Trish replied. 'What that means is that you sit behind the driver and get that authentic outback aroma.'

Otto threw Trish a dirty look and walked out. On entering the usually shabby back room he did a double-take. The room was filled with brand new video games and a giant TV screen, and Conrad was wearing expensive new clothing.

'I thought you were through with the shoplifting stage,' Otto muttered angrily.

'I didn't nick any of it. It's all mine,' Conrad boasted.

'You stole my opal,' Penelope said crossly.

'It was the Von Meister opal first,' Otto growled.

Bruce looked at Conrad.

'Are you going to tell him that it's magic?' he asked.

'What's magic?' asked Otto.

'It's a magic opal, Uncle Otto,' Conrad explained. 'Bruce is a genie. If you make a wish Bruce will make it come true for you.'

Otto was sure that Conrad had gone totally insane. He wrenched the opal away from the boy.

144

'I wish you'd wake up and get a good grip on yourself,' he muttered.

'I can do that,' Baz announced. This was an easy one and he swatted happily. Next second Conrad yawned and stretched and then grabbed his ears.

'Cute!' Otto said sarcastically. 'I wish had ten thousand bucks in my wallet right now.'

Suddenly Otto felt his back pocket expand. He pulled out his wallet and found it was bursting at the seams, crammed with money.

'Sorry, shop's shut,' Otto said as he bustled into the front office. 'Trish, take the day off.'

Trish looked at him in surprise, took the one measly note that he offered her and left. Otto glared at the startled tourists who were looking at brochures and they too departed.

'Otto, it's my go,' whined Conrad.

'You had plenty of go's in the back room,' Otto grunted. 'I knew this opal was lucky!'

A little later the Von Meisters, Penelope and the genies drove out of town in a luxurious limousine that Otto had wished for.

'Bruce was always so mean to me,' sulked Penelope. 'Every time I wished for something, he somehow twisted the wish.'

'You just haven't got the knack, Pen,' Conrad sneered. 'Bruce is giving Otto and me everything we wish for.'

'Do you want to see our special cave?' Baz asked.

'I don't think that's a good idea,' Bruce said quickly.

'You keep out of this,' Otto ordered. 'What cave, Baz?'

'It's where the opal was first found. There's lots of opals there,' Baz piped up.

Otto looked thoughtful. Maybe he should check it out.

'All right,' he said. 'I wish we were at that cave.'

A second later he stood in the cave. With its swathe of opalescent rock and its Aboriginal art, it was very beautiful. Otto stood in silence thinking deeply.

'This cave is the only place in the world where you can wish yourself inside the opal,' Bruce said, trying to tempt Otto into making a wish.

'Forget it,' Otto mumbled. 'I've been thinking I feel like some of Mossop's shepherd's pie. In fact I wish we were there right now.'

With downcast faces Bruce and Baz swatted and the group found themselves standing in the garden of Townes Downs. The sign on the gate had been changed to 'Meister Downs'. With smug looks on their faces, Otto and Conrad walked up to Diana and Mossop who were admiring the garden.

'I reckon we should dig all this up and put in a pool and a spa,' Conrad said smirkingly.

'What are you talking about?' Mossop demanded.

'There's been a change of ownership,' Otto explained.

'You're moving out and we're moving in,' Conrad added.

Penelope went to her room to pack her things. While Conrad watched with an unpleasant smirk on his face, she wondered how she could have ever liked him.

'How can anyone be so greedy and selfish?' she asked.

'Practice, dedication and hard work,' Conrad replied casually.

'Natural talent,' added Baz.

Conrad glared at both of them. He wanted to hurry up this business of getting rid of snooty Penelope.

'You want to take all your stuff with you, Pen?' Conrad asked.

'Yes, I suppose so,' Penelope sighed.

'I wish it was all in England,' Conrad ordered.

Baz swatted and Penelope's things disappeared. She looked around sadly. She'd hated being at Townes Downs, but now she was miserable at the thought of leaving it.

In the kitchen Mossop angrily confronted Otto and Conrad.

'You're putting us out of house and home,' she cried. 'And you want me to give you some of my shepherd's pie!'

'Yes, I wish you would,' Otto replied.

Baz swatted and Mossop turned to Otto with a large slice of pie. Suddenly she shoved it right into his face.

'That's it,' Conrad snapped. 'I'm going to send youse all back to where youse came from. It's been nice knowing you, Pen.'

Out on the verandah Bruce and Diana gazed at each other then closed their eyes as they moved towards each other to kiss. Bruce leaned forward and fell flat on his face. Diana had suddenly disappeared.

At Townes Hall in England, Diana miserably sorted through a pile of bills. With Townes Downs gone, she had nothing left but an ancient mansion that needed a lot of work, and a mountain of bills that she couldn't pay.

'Oh, Mossie,' she sighed. 'What am I going to do?'

'There's always Lord Akryngton-Smythe, the richest man in Wiltshire,' Mossop reminded her.

Diana pulled a face. She didn't want to marry Bubbles, but it might be the only solution. As soon as he heard that she was back, he came visiting. She greeted him in the library.

'I've finally realised why we didn't get married, why it didn't work out,' he told her solemnly. 'My money got in the way.'

Diana looked startled and Bubbles continued.

'If you marry me, I make this solemn vow that I will never, ever give you any of my money. Brilliant, isn't it? I can see why you're looking so stunned.'

'Actually, I was thinking about Penelope,' Diana murmured. 'I can't afford to send her to her old school any more.'

'Oh no,' Bubbles cried.

'She's frightened she'll lose her friends. They've been together since Grade One, but the school fees are so crippling.'

'Don't worry about that,' Bubbles said staunchly. 'Her real friends will stick by her.'

Penelope gasped in surprise as she disappeared and then gasped again as she reappeared in the driveway of Townes Downs. The old weatherboard house had been replaced by

148

a brick veneer monstrosity. Otto and Conrad had completely transformed the place. She found them relaxing in the spa while Bruce lazed nearby in the new pool.

'I'm bored,' grumbled Otto. He'd been placing bets on horse races, but it wasn't any fun when he could wish for his horses to win.

'G'day, Penelope,' Baz cried, obviously pleased to see her.

'We were feeling a bit bored so I thought I'd bring you here and rub your face in it,' Conrad explained. 'What do you think? Me and Otto designed the whole thing ourselves.'

'You don't say,' said Penelope, pulling a face. She thought the whole thing was in very bad taste.

Bruce was almost asleep as he drifted comfortably around the swimming pool on a li-lo.

'It's been all go since you left,' he yawned. 'I'm all wished out. How's your mum?'

'It looks like we might have to sell Townes Hall,' Penelope said darkly.

'Hey Otto,' Conrad nudged his uncle. 'D'you wanna buy a mansion in England?'

'Nah, I can't be bothered. I'm bored,' Otto complained. 'I wish for a lot of ladies to love and adore me.'

Bruce swatted and Otto handed the opal to Conrad.

Conrad thought about wishing for the mansion, just to be mean to Penelope. But then he thought about what he really wanted.

'I want to be wealthy and famous, like a superstar,' he said holding the opal. 'That's my wish.'

Bruce swatted.

'Your fame is spreading while we speak,' he said.

'Bewdy! Pen, I s'pose I better send you back to England,' Conrad drawled. 'I wish . . .'

'Wait,' Penelope cried. 'Perhaps you should keep me here as genie consultant. These chaps can be very tricky, you know.'

'We don't need any consultants,' Otto barked gruffly. ·

'Exactly,' smirked Conrad. 'See you, Pen.'

But before Conrad could wish Penelope away, Trish arrived with a bunch of female tourists who gazed lovingly at Otto.

'We'd like to look at the wildflowers in the desert,' a beautiful girl said. 'Otto, we wondered if you'd guide us. It'd be so romantic.'

'I'm not in the tour business any more,' Otto replied with a smug smile. 'But it would be my pleasure.'

'Hi, Conrad,' Trish called. 'I've been reading all about you in the newspapers. You're so famous now.'

'Wow,' muttered Conrad. 'I'm famous already!'

'Of course,' said Penelope. 'You're huge in England.'

Bruce looked at Penelope suspiciously, guessing she was up to something.

'Why don't you come and see for yourself, Conrad?' Penelope said sweetly. 'It's only a wish away.'

Conrad couldn't resist. Bruce swatted and Conrad quickly found himself at the impressive entrance to Townes Hall.

'Personal appearances?' Conrad said, talking on his mobile phone to his press agent. 'Yeah, I love them.'

Penelope, Bruce and Baz were shocked to see Diana and Mossop supervising two removalists, packing Townes Hall's furniture into a huge van.

'Penelope, there you are,' cried Diana. 'I've been looking everywhere for you.'

Diana met Bruce's eyes and started to cry. Penelope hurried inside with her.

'Her ladyship is selling everything,' Mossop explained.

Conrad pouted because no-one was paying him any attention. Then some fans came around the corner and spotted him.

'It's him!' they screamed.

'Can I have your autograph on my arm, please?' begged a fan. 'It's for my sister.'

One of the removalists also asked Conrad for his autograph. Then the paparazzi arrived in droves. Reporters pestered him with questions as the cameras clicked. Conrad was loving every minute of this.

'You have the smelliest feet in the world,' another fan sighed.

'Whaddya mean?' Conrad asked.

'That's why you're so famous,' the girls cried. 'Didn't you know?'

Conrad scowled. Then his mobile phone rang.

'I don't want a book written about me!' Conrad said to the publisher on the phone. 'What do you mean, it's called *The Smell of Fame*? I'll sue!'

Grimly he held the opal. 'I can feel a wish coming on,' he said.

In an empty, echoing room inside Townes Hall, Bruce tried to comfort Diana.

'Don't worry. You've still got a roof over your head. I really like this open, uncluttered feeling,' he said.

'I've sold the building, too,' Diana told him sadly.

'Oh, well.' Bruce didn't know what to say. 'That's a very open feeling then.'

'It's not the end of the world,' Diana said bravely. 'I've still got Penelope and Mossie.'

'Whatever happens, I want you to know that I'll always be here for you,' Bruce said sincerely.

Diana was very touched. She looked away for a moment and when she looked back, Bruce had disappeared.

Conrad looked around and realised he was standing at the entrance of the opal cave.

'What are we doing here?' he asked.

'You said you wanted to come back to Australia. And this is Australia,' Baz replied happily.

'Yeah, but . . .' Conrad began.

'This'd be a good chance to have a look inside the opal,' Bruce said casually. 'Not many people have been there before.'

'You'd be really famous,' Baz prompted.

'Is this some sort of trick?' Conrad asked. He turned to Penelope. 'What do you reckon?'

Baz and Bruce looked at Penelope, wondering if she'd tell Conrad that the genies could wish themselves free once they were inside the opal with their master. Penelope looked at the genies thoughtfully and then at Conrad.

'I think you should give it a go,' she advised.

'All right,' agreed Conrad. 'I wish we could have a look inside the opal.'

Bruce and Baz looked at each other with glee. They swatted rapidly before Conrad could change his mind. They all disappeared, and the opal hung in the air for a moment before it fell to the ground.

Inside the opal the walls glittered red, green, gold and purple. Magically the opal had come inside itself and Conrad stared at it. He knew he was inside the opal, but somehow the opal was lying just in front of him.

'The opal just fell through my hand,' he said in amazement.

He tried to pick it up but couldn't. Bruce picked it up without any trouble at all and it glittered in the palm of his hand. He and Baz yelled with excitement.

'What's going on?' Conrad demanded.

'In here everything is reversed,' Bruce explained. 'This is the only place in the world where we can hold the opal.'

'You tricked me,' Conrad accused angrily.

Penelope glared at him.

'You wouldn't have saved Mummy and Townes Hall, but maybe someone else will.'

She turned to stare meaningfully at Bruce and Baz, who jumped up and down with excitement.

'We're allowed to make one wish. We're going to wish that we're free,' Bruce cried exultantly.

'What about Mummy and Townes Hall?' Penelope pleaded.

Bruce looked stricken. He used his magic powers to see what Diana was doing. Very sadly she was leaving Townes Hall for the last time.

'Penelope has run away, and the new owners need you, Mossie,' she sobbed. 'I've lost everything.'

Bruce hated to see Diana like that, but he looked sadly at Penelope.

'For more than five thousand years I've been a slave,' he explained. 'I can't stand the idea of watching my son carry this burden for another five thousand years.'

'What about Otto and me!' Conrad screamed.

Bruce had a sudden magic vision of Otto. The bus had broken down and the tour was lost in the desert.

'Otto's in trouble,' he told Conrad. 'The bus is bogged in the desert.'

'What about the women?' Penelope asked.

Bruce pulled a face. 'They're showering him with kisses.'

'Poor Otto,' moaned Conrad.

'Poor women,' groaned Penelope.

'This is the one chance we've got to be free,' Bruce said determinedly. 'And we're going to take it.'

'So you're going to leave everyone stranded,' Penelope accused. 'Including poor Mummy.'

'Once we're free I'll do everything humanly possible to help your mother,' Bruce promised.

'What if human help isn't enough?' Penelope cried.

'Her mother!' scoffed Conrad. 'What about Penelope and me, stuck in a lump of Aussie gemstone?'

'Mummy never hurt anyone,' Penelope begged.

'Neither has Otto,' Conrad declared. 'Well, not many people, and he loves his bus.'

'Dad's never hurt anyone either,' Baz chimed in.

Bruce thought about what Baz said. It was true, and he couldn't hurt anyone now. He and Baz looked at each other and thought about Diana. Neither felt right about leaving her in her plight. Both of them really loved her. Bruce made a sudden decision.

'I'll make a deal with you,' he said to Penelope and Conrad. 'You want to save your mother and Otto. So you each get one wish. But then neither of you get to be my master.'

'Who's going to be master then?' Penelope asked.

'Is it a deal or not?' Bruce said firmly.

It was a deal, and Penelope realised how much it had cost him. It had cost him his freedom.

The opal fell through Bruce's hands as they appeared back in the cave. It lay glittering on the ground between Conrad and Penelope.

'You go first,' Penelope offered.

Conrad picked up the opal and rubbed it. He made his wish and all of them found themselves out in the desert. Otto lay on his belly in the dirt, a quivering, sobbing wreck.

'All those women adore me,' he sobbed. 'I don't want to be adored anymore, I can't stand it.'

'It's all right,' Bruce soothed. 'They think you're a total scumbucket.'

'Really!' cried Otto.

155

'Come on, you useless tub of lard,' Trish bellowed. The bus was ready to go.

'Get in the bus, you mongrels!' Otto shouted happily as he rose to his feet.

'Here you go, Pen,' Conrad said with a smile as he passed the opal to Penelope. Penelope held it tight and closed her eyes.

Lady Diana Townes huddled in a sheltered spot under a bridge on the Thames river, all her possessions beside her in an old shopping trolley. She looked poor, shabby and lonely. But when she saw Penelope, her eyes lit up.

'Penelope! I thought you'd run away!' she cried.

Penelope hugged her.

'I want you to have this,' she said handing her the opal. 'It's very lucky.'

Diana rubbed it and admired its beauty.

'You've rubbed the opal in your hand. Your every wish is our command,' Baz told her.

'Baz, you're so sweet,' Diana said, opening her arms to give the little boy a cuddle. Bruce smiled at her and Diana smiled back.

Townes Hall was saved, but Diana and Penelope, Bruce and Baz spent most of their time at Townes Downs. Bruce didn't tell Diana that he was a genie. He hoped that one day he'd go back inside the opal, become free and marry her. Diana wore the opal around her neck and found that it kept bringing good luck. Somehow all her wishes came true.

Penelope found that she liked Australia now. And she liked Bruce and Baz too. She didn't have the opal any more, but she was happier than she'd ever been. And that, she decided, was just magic.

Also available from BBC Books:

The New Adventures of Superman:
EXILE

M. J. Friedman

"With Superman out of action, we can rule Metropolis!"

Criminal genius, Thaddeus Killgrave, has turned
Superman into the carrier of a deadly virus –
so deadly that it's capable of wiping out the world's
population. As Superman is forced to go into
isolation, Killgrave's thieving associates
ransack the streets of Metropolis.

Clark Kent and Superman may be out of action.
But Lois Lane is working against the clock
to save the Man of Steel – and the human race –
from permanent exile.

A brand-new story of action, romance and adventure,
featuring eight pages of photographs from the hit
BBC TV series.

Priced £2.99 and available from all good bookshops.

Also available from BBC Books:

The New Adventures of Superman:
DEADLY GAMES

M. J. Friedman

"Somebody's out to get me..."

Janna Leighton, a beautiful heiress with a social
conscience unveils a plan to invest millions of dollars in
Metropolis's disadvantaged communities. But as she
publicizes these investments with a series of sporting
contests, she becomes the target of assassins.

With Clark Kent by Janna's side, Superman is able to
keep an eye out for the heires., But Lois Lane doesn't
like to be left out in the cold – especially when it's
Clark freezing her out. Pretty soon, Lois finds herself
caught up in something almost too hot to handle,
playing the deadliest of games.

A brand-new story of action, romance and adventure,
featuring eight pages of photographs from the hit
BBC TV series.

Priced £2.99 and available from all good bookshops.

Also available from BBC Books:

The New Adventures of Superman:
HEAT WAVE

M. J. Friedman

The temperature's rising...

Tempers are reaching boiling point. The hottest summer
on record hits Metropolis and Clark Kent as Superman
is working overtime trying to keep things cool.

When it appears that someone's trying to sabotage a
high-budget action film, Lois Lane goes undercover.
As she closes in on the hottest scoop of the year,
Superman has some pretty tough choices to make –
and if he doesn't make the right ones,
Metropolis could go up in flames.

A brand-new story of action, romance and adventure,
featuring eight pages of photographs from the hit
BBC TV series.

Priced £2.99 and available from all good bookshops.